THE LAST BATTLE

"Never in all my days have I seen such terrible things written in the skies as there have been nightly since this year began," said Roonwit the Centaur.

Indeed, when Jill and Eustace are thrown by a great jerk into Narnia, they discover everything in the most dreadful state of confusion and doubt. Shift, the cleverest, ugliest and most wrinkled of apes, has persuaded poor gullible Puzzle the donkey to wear a lion-skin and pose as Aslan. So when imposter Aslan starts to give terrible orders, the animals and dwarfs are at sixes and sevens about what to do and whom to believe. Now, Tirian, King of Narnia, must act swiftly before the animals are corrupted altogether and the harmony of the kingdom completely destroyed. What a wonderful surprise it is when Peter, Edmund and Lucy join Jill and Eustace to help Tirian in the great battle to decide once and for all the future of the once glorious kingdom of Narnia.

THE CHRONICLES OF NARNIA
are all available in Lions

C. S. LEWIS

The Last Battle

illustrated by
Pauline Baynes

DIAMOND
BOOKS

An Imprint of HarperCollinsPublishers

First published by The Bodley Head 1956
First published in Lions 1980

This edition published 1996
by Diamond Books
A division of HarperCollins Publishers
77-85 Fulham Palace Road
Hammersmith, London W6 8JB

Printed and bound in Great Britain

CONTENTS

CHAPTER ONE

BY CALDRON POOL

In the last days of Narnia, far up to the west beyond Lantern Waste and close beside the great waterfall, there lived an Ape. He was so old that no one could remember when he had first come to live in those parts, and he was the cleverest, ugliest, most wrinkled Ape you can imagine. He had a little house, built of wood and thatched with leaves, up in the fork of a great tree, and his name was Shift. There were very few Talking Beasts or Men or Dwarfs, or people of any sort, in that part of the wood, but Shift had one friend and neighbour who was a donkey called Puzzle. At least they both said they were friends, but from the way things went on you might have thought Puzzle was more like Shift's servant than his friend. He did all the work. When they went together to the river, Shift filled the big skin bottles with water but it was Puzzle who carried them back. When they wanted anything from the towns further down the river it was Puzzle who went down with empty panniers on his back and came back with the panniers full and heavy. And all the nicest things that Puzzle brought back were eaten by Shift; for as Shift said, "You see, Puzzle, I can't eat grass and thistles like you, so it's only fair I should make it up in other ways." And Puzzle always said, "Of course, Shift, of course. I see that." Puzzle never complained, because he knew that Shift was far cleverer than himself and he thought it was very kind of Shift to be friends with him at all. And if ever Puzzle did try to argue about anything, Shift would always say, "Now, Puzzle, I understand what needs to be done better than you. You know you're not clever, Puzzle." And Puzzle

always said, "No, Shift. It's quite true. I'm *not* clever."
Then he would sigh and do whatever Shift had said.

One morning early in the year the pair of them were out
walking along the shore of Caldron Pool. Caldron Pool is
the big pool right under the cliffs at the western end of
Narnia. The great waterfall pours down into it with a noise
like everlasting thunder, and the River of Narnia flows out
on the other side. The waterfall keeps the Pool always
dancing and bubbling and churning round and round as if
it were on the boil, and that of course is how it got its name
of Caldron Pool. It is liveliest in the early spring when the
waterfall is swollen with all the snow that has melted off
the mountains from up beyond Narnia in the Western Wild
from which the river comes. And as they looked at Caldron
Pool Shift suddenly pointed with his dark, skinny finger
and said,

"Look! What's that?"

"What's what?" said Puzzle.

"That yellow thing that's just come down the waterfall.
Look! There it is again, it's floating. We must find out
what it is."

"Must we?" said Puzzle.

"Of course we must," said Shift. "It may be something
useful. Just hop into the Pool like a good fellow and fish it
out. Then we can have a proper look at it."

"Hop into the Pool?" said Puzzle, twitching his long
ears.

"Well how are we to get it if you don't?" said the Ape.

"But – but," said Puzzle, "wouldn't it be better if *you*
went in? Because, you see, it's you who wants to know
what it is, and I don't much. And you've got hands, you
see. You're as good as a Man or a Dwarf when it comes to
catching hold of things. I've only got hoofs."

"Really, Puzzle," said Shift, "I didn't think you'd ever say a thing like that. I didn't think it of you, really."

"Why, what have I said wrong?" said the Ass, speaking in rather a humble voice, for he saw that Shift was very deeply offended. "All I meant was —"

"Wanting *me* to go into the water," said the Ape. "As if you didn't know perfectly well what weak chests Apes always have and how easily they catch cold! Very well. I *will* go in. I'm feeling cold enough already in this cruel wind. But I'll go in. I shall probably die. Then you'll be sorry." And Shift's voice sounded as if he was just going to burst into tears.

"Please don't, please don't, please don't," said Puzzle, half braying, and half talking. "I never meant anything of the sort, Shift, really I didn't. You know how stupid I am and how I can't think of more than one thing at a time. I'd forgotten about your weak chest. Of course I'll go in. You mustn't think of doing it yourself. Promise me you won't, Shift."

So Shift promised, and Puzzle went cloppety-clop on his four hoofs round the rocky edge of the Pool to find a place where he could get in. Quite apart from the cold it was no joke getting into that quivering and foaming water, and Puzzle had to stand and shiver for a whole minute before he made up his mind to do it. But then Shift called out from behind him and said: "Perhaps I'd better do it after all, Puzzle." And when Puzzle heard that he said, "No, no. You promised. I'm in now," and in he went.

A great mass of foam got him in the face and filled his mouth with water and blinded him. Then he went under altogether for a few seconds, and when he came up again he was in quite another part of the Pool. Then the swirl caught him and carried him round and round and faster and faster till it took him right under the waterfall itself, and the force of the water plunged him down, deep down, so that he thought he would never be able to hold his breath till he came up again. And when he had come up and when at last he got somewhere near the thing he was trying to catch, it sailed away from him till it too got under the fall and was forced down to the bottom. When it came up again it was further from him than ever. But at last, when he was almost tired to death, and bruised all over and numb with cold, he succeeded in gripping the thing with his teeth. And out he came carrying it in front of him and getting his front hoofs tangled up in it, for it was as big as a large hearthrug, and it was very heavy and cold and slimy.

He flung it down in front of Shift and stood dripping and shivering and trying to get his breath back. But the Ape never looked at him or asked him how he felt. The Ape was too busy going round and round the Thing and spreading it out and patting it and smelling it. Then a wicked gleam came into his eye and he said:

"It is a lion's skin."

"Ee – auh – auh – oh, is it?" gasped Puzzle.

"Now I wonder . . . I wonder . . . I wonder," said Shift to himself, for he was thinking very hard.

"I wonder who killed the poor lion," said Puzzle presently. "It ought to be buried. We must have a funeral."

"Oh, it wasn't a Talking Lion," said Shift. "You needn't bother about *that*. There are no Talking Beasts up beyond the Falls, up in the Western Wild. This skin must have belonged to a dumb, wild lion."

This, by the way, was true. A Hunter, a Man, had killed and skinned this lion somewhere up in the Western Wild several months before. But that doesn't come into this story.

"All the same, Shift," said Puzzle, "even if the skin only belonged to a dumb, wild lion, oughtn't we to give it a decent burial? I mean, aren't all lions rather – well, rather solemn? Because of you know Who. Don't you see?"

"Don't you start getting ideas into your head, Puzzle," said Shift. "Because, you know, thinking isn't your strong point. We'll make this skin into a fine warm winter coat for you."

"Oh, I don't think I'd like that," said the Donkey. "It

would look – I mean, the other Beasts might think – that is to say, I shouldn't feel –"

"What are you talking about?" said Shift, scratching himself the wrong way up as Apes do.

"I don't think it would be respectful to the Great Lion, to Aslan himself, if an ass like me went about dressed up in a lion-skin," said Puzzle.

"Now don't stand arguing, please," said Shift. "What does an ass like you know about things of that sort? You know you're no good at thinking, Puzzle, so why don't you let me do your thinking for you? Why don't you treat me as I treat you? I don't think I can do everything. I know you're better at some things than I am. That's why I let you go into the Pool; I knew you'd do it better than me. But why can't I have my turn when it comes to something I *can* do and you can't? Am I never to be allowed to do anything? Do be fair. Turn and turn about."

"Oh, well, of course, if you put it that way," said Puzzle.

"I tell you what," said Shift. "You'd better take a good brisk trot down river as far as Chippingford and see if they have any oranges or bananas."

"But I'm so tired, Shift," pleaded Puzzle.

"Yes, but you are very cold and wet," said the Ape. "You want something to warm you up. A brisk trot would be just the thing. Besides, it's market day at Chippingford today." And then of course Puzzle said he would go.

As soon as he was alone Shift went shambling along, sometimes on two paws and sometimes on four, till he reached his own tree. Then he swung himself up from branch to branch, chattering and grinning all the time, and went into his little house. He found needle and thread and a big pair of scissors there; for he was a clever Ape and the

Dwarfs had taught him how to sew. He put the ball of thread (it was very thick stuff, more like cord than thread) into his mouth so that his cheek bulged out as if he were sucking a big bit of toffee. He held the needle between his lips and took the scissors in his left paw. Then he came down the tree and shambled across to the lion-skin. He squatted down and got to work.

He saw at once that the body of the lion-skin would be too long for Puzzle and its neck too short. So he cut a good piece out of the body and used it to make a long collar for Puzzle's long neck. Then he cut off the head and sewed the collar in between the head and the shoulders. He put threads on both sides of the skin so that it would tie up under Puzzle's chest and stomach. Every now and then a bird would pass overhead and Shift would stop his work, looking anxiously up. He did not want anyone to see what he was doing. But none of the birds he saw were Talking Birds, so it didn't matter.

Late in the afternoon Puzzle came back. He was not trotting but only plodding patiently along, the way donkeys do.

"There weren't any oranges," he said, "and there weren't any bananas. And I'm very tired." He lay down.

"Come and try on your beautiful new lion-skin coat," said Shift.

"Oh bother that old skin," said Puzzle. "I'll try it on in the morning. I'm too tired tonight."

"You *are* unkind, Puzzle," said Shift. "If *you're* tired what do you think I am? All day long, while you've been having a lovely refreshing walk down the valley, I've been working hard to make you a coat. My paws are so tired I can hardly hold these scissors. And you won't say thank

you – and you won't even look at the coat – and you don't
care – and – and –"

"My dear Shift," said Puzzle getting up at once, "I am so
sorry. I've been horrid. Of course I'd love to try it on. And it
looks simply splendid. Do try it on me at once. Please do."

"Well, stand still then," said the Ape. The skin was very
heavy for him to lift, but in the end, with a lot of pulling
and pushing and puffing and blowing, he got it on to the
donkey. He tied it underneath Puzzle's body and he tied the
legs to Puzzle's legs and the tail to Puzzle's tail. A good deal
of Puzzle's grey nose and face could be seen through the
open mouth of the lion's head. No one who had ever seen a

real lion would have been taken in for a moment. But if someone who had never seen a lion looked at Puzzle in his lion-skin he just might mistake him for a lion, if he didn't come too close, and if the light was not too good, and if Puzzle didn't let out a bray and didn't make any noise with his hoofs.

"You look wonderful, wonderful," said the Ape. "If anyone saw you now, they'd think you were Aslan, the Great Lion, himself."

"That would be dreadful," said Puzzle.

"No it wouldn't," said Shift. "Everyone would do whatever you told them."

"But I don't want to tell them anything."

"But you think of the good we could do!" said Shift. "You'd have me to advise you, you know. I'd think of sensible orders for you to give. And everyone would have to obey us, even the King himself. We would set everything right in Narnia."

"But isn't everything right already?" said Puzzle.

"What!" cried Shift. "Everything right? – when there are no oranges or bananas?"

"Well, you know," said Puzzle, "there aren't many people – in fact, I don't think there's anyone but yourself – who wants those sort of things."

"There's sugar too," said Shift.

"H'm yes," said the Ass. "It would be nice if there was more sugar."

"Well then, that's settled," said the Ape. "You will pretend to be Aslan, and I'll tell you what to say."

"No, no, no," said Puzzle. "Don't say such dreadful things. It would be wrong, Shift. I may be not very clever but I know that much. What would become of us if the real Aslan turned up?"

"I expect he'd be very pleased," said Shift. "Probably he sent us the lion-skin on purpose, so that we could set things to right. Anyway, he never *does* turn up, you know. Not nowadays."

At that moment there came a great thunderclap right overhead and the gound trembled with a small earthquake. Both the animals lost their balance and were flung on their faces.

"There!" gasped Puzzle, as soon as he had breath to speak. "It's a sign, a warning. I knew we were doing something dreadfully wicked. Take this wretched skin off me at once."

"No, no," said the Ape (whose mind worked very quickly). "It's a sign the other way. I was just going to say that if the real Aslan, as you call him, meant us to go on with this, he would send us a thunderclap and an earth-tremor. It was just on the tip of my tongue, only the sign itself came before I could get the words out. You've *got* to do it now, Puzzle. And please don't let us have any more arguing. You know you don't understand these things. What could a donkey know about signs?"

CHAPTER TWO

THE RASHNESS OF THE KING

ABOUT three weeks later the last of the Kings of Narnia sat under the great oak which grew beside the door of his little hunting lodge, where he often stayed for ten days or so in the pleasant spring weather. It was a low, thatched building not far from the Eastern end of Lantern Waste and some way above the meeting of the two rivers. He loved to live there simply and at ease, away from the state and pomp of Cair Paravel, the royal city. His name was King Tirian, and he was between twenty and twenty-five years old; his shoulders were already broad and strong and his limbs full of hard muscle, but his beard was still scanty. He had blue eyes and a fearless, honest face.

There was no one with him that spring morning except his dearest friend, Jewel the Unicorn. They loved each other like brothers and each had saved the other's life in the wars. The lordly beast stood close beside the King's chair, with its neck bent round polishing its blue horn against the creamy whiteness of its flank.

"I cannot set myself to any work or sport today, Jewel," said the King. "I can think of nothing but this wonderful news. Think you we shall hear any more of it today?"

"They are the most wonderful tidings ever heard in our days or our fathers' or our grandfathers' days, Sire," said Jewel, "if they are true."

"How can they choose but be true?" said the King. "It is more than a week ago that the first birds came flying over us saying, Aslan is here, Aslan has come to Narnia again. And after that it was the squirrels. They had not seen him, but they said it was certain he was in the woods. Then came the Stag. He said he had seen him with his own eyes, a great way off, by moonlight, in Lantern Waste. Then came that dark Man with the beard, the merchant from Calormen. The Calormenes care nothing for Aslan as we do; but the man spoke of it as a thing beyond doubt. And there was the Badger last night; he too had seen Aslan."

"Indeed, Sire," answered Jewel, "I believe it all. If I seem not to, it is only that my joy is too great to let my belief settle itself. It is almost too beautiful to believe."

"Yes," said the King with a great sigh, almost a shiver, of delight. "It is beyond all that I ever hoped for in all my life."

"Listen!" said Jewel, putting his head on one side and cocking his ears forward.

"What is it?" asked the King.

"Hoofs, Sire," said Jewel. "A galloping horse. A very heavy horse. It must be one of the Centaurs. And look, there he is."

A great, golden bearded Centaur, with man's sweat on his forehead and horse's sweat on his chestnut flanks, dashed up to the King, stopped, and bowed low. "Hail, King," it cried in a voice as deep as a bull's.

"Ho, there!" said the King, looking over his shoulder towards the door of the hunting lodge. "A bowl of wine for the noble Centaur. Welcome, Roonwit. When you have found your breath you shall tell us your errand."

A page came out of the house carrying a great wooden bowl, curiously carved, and handed it to the Centaur. The Centaur raised the bowl and said,

"I drink first to Aslan and truth, Sire, and secondly to your Majesty."

He finished the wine (enough for six strong men) at one draught and handed the empty bowl back to the page.

"Now, Roonwit," said the King. "Do you bring us more news of Aslan?"

Roonwit looked very grave, frowning a little.

"Sire," he said. "You know how long I have lived and studied the stars; for we Centaurs live longer than you Men, and even longer than your kind, Unicorn. Never in

all my days have I seen such terrible things written in the skies as there have been nightly since this year began. The stars say nothing of the coming of Aslan, nor of peace, nor of joy. I know by my art that there have not been such disastrous conjunctions of the planets for five hundred years. It was already in my mind to come and warn your Majesty that some great evil hangs over Narnia. But last night the rumour reached me that Aslan is abroad in Narnia. Sire, do not believe this tale. It cannot be. The stars never lie, but Men and Beasts do. If Aslan were really coming to Narnia the sky would have foretold it. If he were really come, all the most gracious stars would be assembled in his honour. It is all a lie."

"A lie!" said the King fiercely. "What creature in Narnia or all the world would dare to lie on such a matter?" And, without knowing it, he laid his hand on his sword hilt.

"That I know not, Lord King," said the Centaur. "But I know there are liars on earth; there are none among the stars."

"I wonder," said Jewel, "whether Aslan might not come though all the stars foretold otherwise. He is not the slave of the stars but their Maker. Is it not said in all the old stories that He is not a tame lion."

"Well said, well said, Jewel," cried the King. "Those are the very words: *not a tame lion*. It comes in many tales."

Roonwit had just raised his hand and was leaning forward to say something very earnestly to the King when all three of them turned their heads to listen to a wailing sound that was quickly drawing nearer. The wood was so thick to the West of them that they could not see the newcomer yet. But they could soon hear the words.

"Woe, woe, woe!" called the voice. "Woe for my brothers and sisters! Woe for the holy trees! The woods are laid waste. The axe is loosed against us. We are being felled. Great trees are falling, falling, falling."

With the last "falling" the speaker came in sight. She was like a woman but so tall that her head was on a level with the Centaur's yet she was like a tree too. It is hard to explain if you have never seen a Dryad but quite unmistakable once you have — something different in the colour, the voice, and the hair. King Tirian and the two Beasts knew at once that she was the nymph of a beech tree.

"Justice, Lord King!" she cried. "Come to our aid. Protect your people. They are felling us in Lantern Waste.

Forty great trunks of my brothers and sisters are already on the ground."

"What, Lady! Felling Lantern Waste? Murdering the talking trees?" cried the King, leaping to his feet and drawing his sword. "How dare they? And who dares it? Now, by the Mane of Aslan –"

"A-a-a-h," gasped the Dryad shuddering as if in pain – shuddering time after time as if under repeated blows. Then all at once she fell sideways as suddenly as if both her feet had been cut from under her. For a second they saw her lying dead on the grass and then she vanished. They knew what had happened. Her tree, miles away, had been cut down.

For a moment the King's grief and anger were so great that he could not speak. Then he said:

"Come, friends. We must go up river and find the villains who have done this, with all the speed we may. I will leave not one of them alive."

"Sire, with a good will," said Jewel.

But Roonwit said, "Sire, be wary in your just wrath. There are strange doings on foot. If there should be rebels in arms further up the valley, we three are too few to meet them. If it would please you to wait while –"

"I will not wait the tenth part of a second," said the King. "But while Jewel and I go forward, do you gallop as hard as you may to Cair Paravel. Here is my ring for your token. Get me a score of men-at-arms, all well mounted, and a score of Talking Dogs, and ten Dwarfs (let them all be fell archers), and a Leopard or so, and Stonefoot the Giant. Bring all these after us as quickly as may be."

"With a good will, Sire," said Roonwit. And at once he turned and galloped Eastward down the valley.

The King strode on at a great pace, sometimes muttering to himself and sometimes clenching his fists. Jewel walked beside him, saying nothing; so there was no sound between them but the faint jingle of a rich gold chain that hung round the Unicorn's neck and the noise of two feet and four hoofs.

They soon reached the River and turned up it where there was a grassy road: they had the water on their left and the forest on their right. Soon after that they came to the place where the ground grew rougher and thick wood came down to the water's edge. The road, what there was of it, now ran on the Southern bank and they had to ford the River to reach it. It was up to Tirian's arm-pits, but Jewel (who had four legs and was therefore steadier) kept on his right so as to break the force of the current, and Tirian put his strong arm round the Unicorn's strong neck and they both got safely over. The King was still so angry that he hardly noticed the cold of the water. But of course he dried his sword very carefully on the shoulder of his cloak, which was the only dry part of him, as soon as they came to shore.

They were now going Westward with the River on their right and Lantern Waste straight ahead of them. They had not gone more than a mile when they both stopped and both spoke at the same moment. The King said "What have we here?" and Jewel said "Look!"

"It is a raft," said King Tirian.

And so it was. Half a dozen splendid tree-trunks, all newly cut and newly lopped of their branches, had been lashed together to make a raft, and were gliding swiftly down the river. On the front of the raft there was a water rat with a pole to steer it.

"Hey! Water-Rat! What are you about?" cried the King.

"Taking logs down to sell to the Calormenes, Sire," said the Rat, touching his ear as he might have touched his cap if he had had one.

"Calormenes!" thundered Tirian. "What do you mean? Who gave order for these trees to be felled?"

The River flows so swiftly at that time of the year that the raft had already glided past the King and Jewel. But the Water-Rat looked back over its shoulder and shouted out:

"The Lion's orders, Sire. Aslan himself." He added something more but they couldn't hear it.

The King and the Unicorn stared at one another and both looked more frightened than they had ever been in any battle.

"Aslan," said the King at last, in a very low voice. "Aslan. Could it be true? *Could* he be felling the holy trees and murdering the Dryads?"

"Unless the Dryads have all done something dreadfully wrong –" murmured Jewel.

"But selling them to Calormenes!" said the King. "Is it possible?"

"I don't know," said Jewel miserably. "He's not a *tame* lion."

"Well," said the King at last, "we must go on and take the adventure that comes to us."

"It is the only thing left for us to do, Sire," said the Unicorn. He did not see at the moment how foolish it was for two of them to go on alone; nor did the King. They were too angry to think clearly. But much evil came of their rashness in the end.

Suddenly the King leaned hard on his friend's neck and bowed his head.

"Jewel," he said, "what lies before us? Horrible thoughts arise in my heart. If we had died before today we should have been happy."

"Yes," said Jewel. "We have lived too long. The worst thing in the world has come upon us." They stood like that for a minute or two and then went on.

Before long they could hear the hack-hack-hack of axes falling on timber, though they could see nothing yet because there was a rise of the ground in front of them. When they had reached the top of it they could see right into Lantern Waste itself. And the King's face turned white when he saw it.

Right through the middle of that ancient forest — that forest where the trees of gold and of silver had once grown and where a child from our world had once planted the Tree of Protection — a broad lane had already been opened. It was a hideous lane like a raw gash in the land, full of muddy ruts where felled trees had been dragged down to the river. There was a great crowd of people at work, and a cracking of whips, and horses tugging and straining as they dragged at the logs. The first thing that struck the King and the Unicorn was that about half the people in the crowd were not Talking Beasts but Men. The next thing was that these men were not the fair-haired men of Narnia: they were dark, bearded men from Calormen, that great and cruel country that lies beyond Archenland across the desert to the south. There was no reason, of course, why one should not meet a Calormene or two in Narnia – a merchant or an ambassador – for there was peace between Narnia and Calormen in those days. But Tirian could not understand why there were so many of them: nor why they were cutting down a Narnian forest. He grasped his sword tighter and rolled his cloak round his left arm. They came quickly down among the men.

Two Calormenes were driving a horse which was harnessed to a log. Just as the King reached them the log had got stuck in a bad muddy place.

"Get on, son of sloth! Pull, you lazy pig!" cried the Calormenes, cracking their whips. The horse was already straining himself as hard as he could; his eyes were red and he was covered with foam.

"Work, lazy brute," shouted one of the Calormenes: and as he spoke he struck the horse savagely with his whip. It was then that the really dreadful thing happened.

Up till now Tirian had taken it for granted that the horses which the Calormenes were driving were their own horses; dumb, witless animals like the horses of our own world. And though he hated to see even a dumb horse overdriven, he was of course thinking more about the murder of the Trees. It had never crossed his mind that anyone would dare to harness one of the free Talking Horses of Narnia, much less to use a whip on it. But as that

savage blow fell the horse reared up and said, half
screaming:

"Fool and tyrant! Do you not see I am doing all I can?"

When Tirian knew that the Horse was one of his own
Narnians, there came over him and over Jewel such a rage
that they did not know what they were doing. The King's
sword went up, the Unicorn's horn went down. They
rushed forward together. Next moment both the Calormenes lay dead, the one beheaded by Tirian's sword and
the other gored through the heart by Jewel's horn.

CHAPTER THREE

THE APE IN ITS GLORY

"MASTER Horse, Master Horse," said Tirian as he hastily cut its traces, "how came these aliens to enslave you? Is Narnia conquered? Has there been a battle?"

"No, Sire," panted the horse, "Aslan is here. It is all by his orders. He has commanded –"

"'Ware danger, King," said Jewel. Tirian looked up and saw that Calormenes (mixed with a few Talking Beasts) were beginning to run towards them from every direction. The two dead men had died without a cry and so it had taken a moment before the rest of the crowd knew what had happened. But now they did. Most of them had naked scimitars in their hands.

"Quick. On my back," said Jewel.

The King flung himself astride of his old friend who turned and galloped away. He changed direction twice or thrice as soon as they were out of sight of their enemies, crossed a stream, and shouted without slackening his pace, "Whither away, Sire? To Cair Paravel?"

"Hold hard, friend," said Tirian. "Let me off." He slid off the Unicorn's back and faced him.

"Jewel," said the King. "We have done a dreadful deed."

"We were sorely provoked," said Jewel.

"But to leap on them unawares – without defying them – while they were unarmed – faugh! We are two murderers, Jewel. I am dishonoured forever."

Jewel drooped his head. He too was ashamed.

"And then," said the King, "the Horse said it was by Aslan's orders. The Rat said the same. They all say Aslan is here. How if it were true?"

"But, Sire, how *could* Aslan be commanding such dreadful things?"

"He is not a *tame* lion," said Tirian. "How should we know what he would do? We, who are murderers. Jewel, I will go back. I will give up my sword and put myself in the hands of these Calormenes and ask that they bring me before Aslan. Let him do justice on me."

"You will go to your death, then," said Jewel.

"Do you think I care if Aslan dooms me to death?" said the King. "That would be nothing, nothing at all. Would it not be better to be dead than to have this horrible fear that Aslan has come and is not like the Aslan we have believed in and longed for? It is as if the sun rose one day and were a black sun."

"I know," said Jewel. "Or as if you drank water and it were *dry* water. You are in the right, Sire. This is the end of all things. Let us go and give ourselves up."

"There is no need for both of us to go."

"If ever we loved one another, let me go with you now," said the Unicorn. "If you are dead and if Aslan is not Aslan, what life is left for me?"

They turned and walked back together, shedding bitter tears.

As soon as they came to the place where the work was going on the Calormenes raised a cry and came towards them with their weapons in hand. But the King held out his sword with the hilt towards them and said:

"I who was King of Narnia and am now a dishonoured knight give myself up to the justice of Aslan. Bring me before him."

"And I give myself up too," said Jewel.

Then the dark men came round them in a thick crowd, smelling of garlic and onions, their white eyes flashing dreadfully in their brown faces. They put a rope halter round Jewel's neck. They took the King's sword away and tied his hands behind his back. One of the Calormenes, who had a helmet instead of a turban and seemed to be in command, snatched the gold circlet off Tirian's head and hastily put it away somewhere among his clothes. They led the two prisoners uphill to a place where there was a big clearing. And this was what the prisoners saw.

At the centre of the clearing, which was also the highest point of the hill, there was a little hut like a stable, with a thatched roof. Its door was shut. On the grass in front of the door there sat an Ape. Tirian and Jewel, who had been expecting to see Aslan and had heard nothing about an Ape yet, were very bewildered when they saw it. The Ape was of course Shift himself, but he looked ten times uglier than when he lived by Caldron Pool, for he was now dressed up. He was wearing a scarlet jacket which did not fit him very well, having been made for a dwarf. He had jewelled slippers on his hind paws which would not stay on properly because, as you know, the hind paws of an Ape are really like hands. He wore what seemed to be a paper crown on his head. There was a great pile of nuts beside him and he kept cracking nuts with his jaws and spitting out the shells. And he also kept on pulling up the scarlet jacket to scratch himself. A great number of Talking Beasts stood facing him, and nearly every face in that crowd looked miserably worried and bewildered. When they saw who the prisoners were they all groaned and whimpered.

"O Lord Shift, mouthpiece of Aslan," said the chief Calormene. "We bring you prisoners. By our skill and courage and by the permission of the great god Tash we have taken alive these two desperate murderers."

"Give me that man's sword," said the Ape. So they took

the King's sword and handed it, with the sword-belt and all, to the monkey. And he hung it round his own neck: and it made him look sillier than ever.

"We'll see about those two later," said the Ape, spitting out a shell in the direction of the two prisoners. "I got some other business first. They can wait. Now listen to me, everyone. The first thing I want to say is about nuts. Where's that Head Squirrel got to?"

"Here, Sir," said a red squirrel, coming forward and making a nervous little bow.

"Oh you are, are you?" said the Ape with a nasty look. "Now attend to me. I want – I mean, Aslan wants – some more nuts. These you've brought aren't anything like enough. You must bring some more, do you hear? Twice as many. And they've got to be here by sunset tomorrow, and there mustn't be any bad ones or any small ones among them."

A murmur of dismay ran through the other squirrels, and the Head Squirrel plucked up courage to say:

"Please, would Aslan himself speak to us about it? If we might be allowed to see him –"

"Well you won't," said the Ape. "He may be very kind (though it's a lot more than most of you deserve) and come out for a few minutes tonight. Then you can all have a look at him. But he will *not* have you all crowding round him and pestering him with questions. Anything you want to say to him will be passed on through me: if I think it's worth bothering him about. In the meantime all you squirrels had better go and see about the nuts. And make sure they are here by tomorrow evening or, my word! you'll catch it."

The poor squirrels all scampered away as if a dog were after them. This new order was terrible news for them. The nuts they had carefully hoarded for the winter had nearly all been eaten by now; and of the few that were left they had already given the Ape far more than they could spare.

Then a deep voice – it belonged to a great tusked and shaggy Boar – spoke from another part of the crowd.

"But *why* can't we see Aslan properly and talk to him?" it said. "When he used to appear in Narnia in the old days everyone could talk to him face to face."

"Don't you believe it," said the Ape. "And even if it was true, times have changed. Aslan says he's been far too soft with you before, do you see? Well, he isn't going to be soft any more. He's going to lick you into shape this time. He'll teach you to think he's a tame lion!"

A low moaning and whimpering was heard among the Beasts; and, after that, a dead silence which was more miserable still.

"And now there's another thing you got to learn," said the Ape. "I hear some of you are saying I'm an Ape. Well, I'm not. I'm a Man. If I look like an Ape, that's because I'm so very old: hundreds and hundreds of years old. And it's because I'm so old that I'm so wise. And it's because I'm so wise that I'm the only one Aslan is ever going to speak to. He can't be bothered talking to a lot of stupid animals. He'll tell me what you've got to do, and I'll tell the rest of you. And take my advice, and see you do it in double quick time, for he doesn't mean to stand any nonsense."

There was a dead silence except for the noise of a very young badger crying and its mother trying to make it keep quiet.

"And now here's another thing," the Ape went on, fitting a fresh nut into its cheek, "I hear some of the horses are saying, Let's hurry up and get this job of carting timber over as quickly as we can, and then we'll be free again. Well, you can get that idea out of your heads at once. And not only the Horses either. Everybody who can work is going to be made to work in future. Aslan has it all settled with the King of Calormen – The Tisroc, as our dark faced friends the Calormenes call him. All you Horses and Bulls and Donkeys are to be sent down into Calormen to work for your living – pulling and carrying the way horses and such-like do in other countries. And all you digging animals like Moles and Rabbits and Dwarfs are going down to work in The Tisroc's mines. And –"

"No, no, no," howled the Beasts. "It can't be true. Aslan would never sell us into slavery to the King of Calormen."

"None of that! Hold your noise!" said the Ape with a snarl. "Who said anything about slavery? You won't be slaves. You'll be paid – very good wages too. That is to say, your pay will be paid into Aslan's treasury and he will use it all for everybody's good." Then he glanced, and almost winked, at the chief Calormene. The Calormene bowed and replied, in the pompous Calormene way:

"Most sapient Mouthpiece of Aslan, The Tisroc (may-he-live-forever) is wholly of one mind with your lordship in this judicious plan."

"There! You see!" said the Ape. "It's all arranged. And all for your own good. We'll be able, with the money you earn, to make Narnia a country worth living in. There'll be oranges and bananas pouring in – and roads and big cities and schools and offices and whips and muzzles and saddles and cages and kennels and prisons – Oh, everything."

"But we don't want all those things," said an old Bear. "We want to be free. And we want to hear Aslan speak himself."

"Now don't you start arguing," said the Ape, "for it's a thing I won't stand. I'm a Man: you're only a fat, stupid old Bear. What do you know about freedom? You think freedom means doing what you like. Well, you're wrong. That isn't true freedom. True freedom means doing what I tell you."

"H-n-n-h," grunted the Bear and scratched its head; it found this sort of thing hard to understand.

"Please, please," said the high voice of a woolly lamb, who was so young that everyone was surprised he dared to speak at all.

"What is it now?" said the Ape. "Be quick."

"Please," said the Lamb, "I can't understand. What have we to do with the Calormenes? We belong to Aslan. They belong to Tash. They have a god called Tash. They say he has four arms and the head of a vulture. They kill Men on his altar. I don't believe there's any such person as Tash. But if there was, how could Aslan be friends with him?"

All the animals cocked their heads sideways and all their bright eyes flashed towards the Ape. They knew it was the best question anyone had asked yet.

The Ape jumped up and spat at the Lamb.

"Baby!" he hissed. "Silly little bleater! Go home to your mother and drink milk. What do you understand of such things? But the others, listen. Tash is only another name for Aslan. All that old idea of us being right and the Calormenes wrong is silly. We know better now. The Calormenes use different words but we all mean the same thing. Tash and Aslan are only two different names for you know Who. That's why there can never be any quarrel between them. Get that into your heads, you stupid brutes. Tash is Aslan: Aslan is Tash."

You know how sad your own dog's face can look sometimes. Think of that and then think of all the faces of those Talking Beasts — all those honest, humble, bewildered Birds, Bears, Badgers, Rabbits, Moles, and Mice — all far sadder than that. Every tail was down, every whisker drooped. It would have broken your heart with very pity to see their faces. There was only one who did not look at all unhappy.

It was a ginger Cat – a great big Tom in the prime of life – who sat bolt upright with his tail curled round his toes, in the very front row of all the Beasts. He had been staring hard at the Ape and the Calormene captain all the time and had never once blinked his eyes.

"Excuse me," said the Cat very politely, "but this interests me. Does your friend from Calormen say the same?"

"Assuredly," said the Calormene. "The enlightened Ape – Man, I mean – is in the right. *Aslan* means neither less nor more than *Tash*."

"Especially, Aslan means *no more* than Tash?" suggested the Cat.

"No more at all," said the Calormene, looking the Cat straight in the face.

"Is that good enough for you, Ginger?" said the Ape.

"Oh certainly," said Ginger coolly. "Thank you very much. I only wanted to be quite clear. I think I am beginning to understand."

Up till now the King and Jewel had said nothing: they were waiting until the Ape should bid them speak, for they thought it was no use interrupting. But now, as Tirian looked round on the miserable faces of the Narnians, and saw how they would all believe that Aslan and Tash were one and the same, he could bear it no longer.

"Ape," he cried with a great voice, "you lie damnably. You lie like a Calormene. You lie like an Ape."

He meant to go on and ask how the terrible god Tash who fed on the blood of his people could possibly be the same as the good Lion by whose blood all Narnia was saved. If he had been allowed to speak, the rule of the Ape might have ended that day; the Beasts might have seen the truth and thrown the Ape down. But before he could say another word two Calormenes struck him in the mouth with all their force, and a third, from behind, kicked his feet from under him. And as he fell, the Ape squealed in rage and terror.

"Take him away. Take him away. Take him where he cannot hear us, nor we hear him. There tie him to a tree. I will – I mean, Aslan will – do justice on him later."

CHAPTER FOUR

WHAT HAPPENED THAT NIGHT

THE King was so dizzy from being knocked down that he hardly knew what was happening until the Calormenes untied his wrists and put his arms straight down by his sides and set him with his back against an ash tree. Then they bound ropes round his ankles and his knees and his waist and his chest and left him there. What worried him worst at the moment – for it is often little things that are hardest to stand – was that his lip was bleeding where they had hit him and he couldn't wipe the little trickle of blood away although it tickled him.

From where he was he could still see the little stable on the top of the hill and the Ape sitting in front of it. He could just hear the Ape's voice still going on and, every now and then, some answer from the crowd, but he could not make out the words.

"I wonder what they've done to Jewel," thought the King.

Presently the crowd of beasts broke up and began going away in different directions. Some passed close to Tirian. They looked at him as if they were both frightened and sorry to see him tied up but none of them spoke. Soon they had all gone and there was silence in the wood. Then hours and hours went past and Tirian became first very thirsty and then very hungry; and as the afternoon dragged on and turned into evening, he became cold too. His back was very sore. The sun went down and it began to be twilight.

When it was almost dark Tirian heard a light pitter-patter of feet and saw some small creatures coming towards him. The three on the left were Mice, and there

was a Rabbit in the middle: on the right were two Moles.
Both these were carrying little bags on their backs which
gave them a curious look in the dark so that at first he
wondered what kind of beasts they were. Then, in a
moment, they were all standing up on their hind legs,
laying their cool paws on his knees and giving his knees
snuffly animal kisses. (They could reach his knees because
Narnian Talking Beasts of that sort are bigger than the
dumb beasts of the same kind in England.)

"Lord King! dear Lord King," said their shrill voices,
"we are so sorry for you. We daren't untie you because
Aslan might be angry with us. But we've brought you your
supper."

At once the first Mouse climbed nimbly up till he was

perched on the rope that bound Tirian's chest and was wrinkling his blunt nose in front of Tirian's face. Then the second Mouse climbed up and hung on just below the first Mouse. The other beasts stood on the ground and began handing things up.

"Drink, Sire, and then you'll find you are able to eat," said the topmost Mouse, and Tirian found that a little wooden cup was being held to his lips. It was only the size of an egg cup so that he had hardly tasted the wine in it before it was empty. But then the Mouse passed it down and the others re-filled it and it was passed up again and Tirian emptied it a second time. In this way they went on till he had quite a good drink, which was all the better for coming in little doses, for that is more thirst-quenching than one long draught.

"Here is cheese, Sire," said the first Mouse, "but not very much, for fear it would make you too thirsty." And after the cheese they fed him with oat-cakes and fresh butter, and then with some more wine.

"Now hand up the water," said the first Mouse, "and I'll wash the King's face. There is blood on it."

Then Tirian felt something like a tiny sponge dabbing his face, and it was most refreshing.

"Little friends," said Tirian, "how can I thank you for all this?"

"You needn't, you needn't," said the little voices. "What else could we do? *We* don't want any other King. We're your people. If it was only the Ape and the Calormenes who were against you we would have fought till we were cut into pieces before we'd let them tie you up. We would, we would indeed. But we can't go against Aslan."

"Do you think it really is Aslan?" asked the King.

"Oh yes, yes," said the Rabbit. "He came out of the stable last night. We all saw him."

"What was he like?" said the King.

"Like a terrible, great Lion, to be sure," said one of the Mice.

"And you think it is really Aslan who is killing the Wood-Nymphs and making you all slaves to the King of Calormen?"

"Ah, that's bad, isn't it?" said the second Mouse. "It would have been better if we'd died before all this began. But there's no doubt about it. Everyone says it is Aslan's orders. And we've seen him. We didn't think Aslan would be like that. Why, we – we *wanted* him to come back to Narnia."

"He seems to have come back very angry this time," said the first Mouse. "We must all have done something dreadfully wrong without knowing it. He must be punishing us for something. But I do think we might be told what it was!"

"I suppose what we're doing now may be wrong," said the Rabbit.

"I don't care if it is," said one of the Moles. "I'd do it again."

But the others said, "Oh hush," and "Do be careful," and then they all said, "We're sorry, dear King, but we must go back now. It would never do for us to be caught here."

"Leave me at once, dear Beasts," said Tirian. "I would not for all Narnia bring any of you into danger."

"Goodnight, goodnight," said the Beasts, rubbing their noses against his knees. "We will come back – if we can." Then they all pattered away and the wood seemed darker and colder and lonelier than it had been before they came.

The stars came out and time went slowly on – imagine how slowly – while that last King of Narnia stood stiff and sore and upright against the tree in his bonds. But at last something happened.

Far away there appeared a red light. Then it disappeared for a moment and came back again, bigger and stronger. Then he could see dark shapes going to and fro on this side of the light and carrying bundles and throwing them down. He knew now what he was looking at. It was a bonfire, newly lit, and people were throwing bundles of brushwood on to it. Presently it blazed up and Tirian could see that it was on the very top of the hill. He could see quite clearly the stable behind it, all lit up in the red glow, and a great crowd of Beasts and Men between the fire and himself. A small figure, hunched up beside the fire, must be the Ape. It was saying something to the crowd, but he could not hear what. Then it went and bowed three times to the ground in front of the door of the stable. Then it got up and opened the door. And something on four legs – something that walked rather stiffly – came out of the stable and stood facing the crowd.

A great wailing or howling went up, so loud that Tirian could hear some of the words.

"Aslan! Aslan! Aslan!" cried the Beasts. "Speak to us. Comfort us. Be angry with us no more."

From where Tirian was he could not make out very clearly what the thing was; but he could see that it was yellow and hairy. He had never seen the Great Lion. He had never seen a common lion. He couldn't be sure that what he saw was not the real Aslan. He had not expected Aslan to look like that stiff thing which stood and said nothing. But how could one be sure? For a moment horrible thoughts went through his mind: then he remembered

the nonsense about Tash and Aslan being the same and knew that the whole thing must be a cheat.

The Ape put his head close up to the yellow thing's head as if he were listening to something it was whispering to him. Then he turned and spoke to the crowd, and the crowd wailed again. Then the yellow thing turned clumsily round and walked – you might almost say, waddled – back into the stable and the Ape shut the door behind it. After that the fire must have been put out for the light vanished quite suddenly, and Tirian was once more alone with the cold and the darkness.

He thought of other Kings who had lived and died in Narnia in old times and it seemed to him that none of them had ever been so unlucky as himself. He thought of his great-grandfather's great-grandfather King Rilian who had been stolen away by a Witch when he was only a young prince and kept hidden for years in the dark caves beneath the land of the Northern Giants. But then it had all come right in the end, for two mysterious children had suddenly appeared from the land beyond the world's end and had rescued him so that he came home to Narnia and had a long and prosperous reign. "It's not like that with me," said Tirian to himself. Then he went further back and thought about Rilian's father, Caspian the Seafarer, whose wicked uncle King Miraz had tried to murder him and how Caspian had fled away into the woods and lived among the Dwarfs. But that story too had all come right in the end: for Caspian also had been helped by children – only there were four of them that time – who came from somewhere beyond the world and fought a great battle and set him on his father's throne. "But it was all long ago," said Tirian to himself. "That sort of thing doesn't happen now." And then he remembered (for he had always been good at history when he was a boy) how those same four children who had helped Caspian had been in Narnia over a thousand years before; and it was then that they had done the most remarkable thing of all. For then they had defeated the terrible White Witch and ended the Hundred Years of Winter, and after that they had reigned (all four of them together) at Cair Paravel, till they were no longer children but great Kings and lovely Queens, and their reign had been the golden age of Narnia. And Aslan had come into that story a lot. He had come into all the other stories too, as Tirian now remembered. "Aslan – and children from another world," thought Tirian. "They have always come in when things were at their worst. Oh, if only they could now."

And he called out "Aslan! Aslan! Aslan! Come and help us now."

But the darkness and the cold and the quietness went on just the same.

"Let *me* be killed," cried the King. "I ask nothing for myself. But come and save all Narnia."

And still there was no change in the night or the wood, but there began to be a kind of change inside Tirian. Without knowing why, he began to feel a faint hope. And he felt somehow stronger. "Oh Aslan, Aslan," he whispered. "If you will not come yourself, at least send me the helpers from beyond the world. Or let me call them. Let my voice carry beyond the world." Then, hardly knowing that he was doing it, he suddenly cried out in a great voice:

"Children! Children! Friends of Narnia! Quick. Come to me. Across the worlds I call you; I Tirian, King of Narnia, Lord of Cair Paravel, and Emperor of the Lone Islands!"

And immediately he was plunged into a dream (if it was a dream) more vivid than any he had had in his life.

He seemed to be standing in a lighted room where seven people sat round a table. It looked as if they had just finished their meal. Two of those people were very old, an old man with a white beard and an old woman with wise, merry, twinkling eyes. He who sat at the right hand of the old man was hardly full grown, certainly younger than Tirian himself, but his face had already the look of a king and a warrior. And you could almost say the same of the other youth who sat at the right hand of the old woman. Facing Tirian across the table sat a fair-haired girl younger than either of these, and on either side of her a boy and girl who were younger still. They were all dressed in what seemed to Tirian the oddest kind of clothes.

But he had no time to think about details like that, for instantly the younger boy and both the girls started to their feet, and one of them gave a little scream. The old woman started and drew in her breath sharply. The old man must have made some sudden movement too for the wine glass which stood at his right hand was swept off the table: Tirian could hear the tinkling noise as it broke on the floor.

Then Tirian realized that these people could see him; they were staring at him as if they saw a ghost. But he noticed that the king-like one who sat at the old man's right never moved (though he turned pale) except that he clenched his hand very tight. Then he said:

"Speak, if you're not a phantom or a dream. You have a Narnian look about you and we are the seven friends of Narnia."

Tirian was longing to speak, and he tried to cry out aloud that he was Tirian of Narnia, in great need of help. But he found (as I have sometimes found in dreams too) that his voice made no noise at all.

The one who had already spoken to him rose to his feet. "Shadow or spirit or whatever you are," he said, fixing his eyes full upon Tirian. "If you are from Narnia, I charge you in the name of Aslan, speak to me. I am Peter the High King."

The room began to swim before Tirian's eyes. He heard the voices of those seven people all speaking at once, and all getting fainter every second, and they were saying things like, "Look! It's fading." "It's melting away." "It's vanishing." Next moment he was wide awake, still tied to the tree, colder and stiffer than ever. The wood was full of the pale, dreary light that comes before sunrise, and he was soaking wet with dew; it was nearly morning.

That waking was about the worst moment he had ever had in his life.

CHAPTER FIVE

HOW HELP CAME TO THE KING

But his misery did not last long. Almost at once there came a bump, and then a second bump, and two children were standing before him. The wood in front of him had been quite empty a second before and he knew they had not come from behind his tree, for he would have heard them. They had in fact simply appeared from nowhere. He saw at a glance that they were wearing the same queer, dingy sort of clothes as the people in his dream; and he saw, at a second glance, that they were the youngest boy and girl out of that party of seven.

"Gosh!" said the boy, "that took one's breath away! I thought –"

"Hurry up and get him untied," said the girl. "We can talk, afterwards." Then she added, turning to Tirian, "I'm sorry we've been so long. We came the moment we could."

While she was speaking the Boy produced a knife from his pocket and was quickly cutting the King's bonds: too quickly, in fact, for the King was so stiff and numb that when the last cord was cut he fell forward on his hands and knees. He couldn't get up again till he had brought some life back into his legs by a good rubbing.

"I say," said the girl. "It was you, wasn't it, who appeared to us that night when we were all at supper? Nearly a week ago."

"A week, fair maid?" said Tirian. "My dream led me into your world scarce ten minutes since."

"It's the usual muddle about times, Pole," said the Boy.

"I remember now," said Tirian. "That too comes in all the old tales. The time of your strange land is different from ours. But if we speak of Time, 'tis time to be gone from here: for my enemies are close at hand. Will you come with me?"

"Of course," said the girl. "It's you we've come to help."

Tirian got to his feet and led them rapidly down hill, Southward and away from the stable. He knew where he meant to go but his first aim was to get to rocky places where they would leave no trail, and his second to cross some water so that they would leave no scent. This took them about an hour's scrambling and wading and while that was going on nobody had any breath to talk. But even so, Tirian kept on stealing glances at his companions. The wonder of walking beside the creatures from another world made him feel a little dizzy: but it also made all the old stories seem far more real than they had ever seemed before . . . anything might happen now.

"Now," said Tirian as they came to the head of a little valley which ran down before them among young birch trees, "we are out of danger of those villains for a space and may walk more easily." The sun had risen, dew-drops were twinkling on every branch, and birds were singing.

"What about some grub? – I mean for you, Sir, we two have had our breakfast," said the Boy.

Tirian wondered very much what he meant by "grub", but when the Boy opened a bulgy satchel which he was carrying and pulled out a rather greasy and squashy packet, he understood. He was ravenously hungry, though he hadn't thought about it till that moment. There were two hard-boiled egg sandwiches, and two cheese sandwiches, and two with some kind of paste in them. If he hadn't been so hungry he wouldn't have thought much of the paste, for that is a sort of food nobody eats in Narnia. By the time he had eaten all six sandwiches they had come

to the bottom of the valley and there they found a mossy cliff with a little fountain bubbling out of it. All three stopped and drank and splashed their hot faces.

"And now," said the girl as she tossed her wet hair back from her forehead, "aren't you going to tell us who you are and why you were tied up and what it's all about?"

"With a good will, damsel," said Tirian. "But we must keep on the march." So while they went on walking he told them who he was and all the things that had happened to him. "And now," he said at the end, "I am going to a certain tower, one of three that were built in my grandsire's time to guard Lantern Waste against certain perilous outlaws who dwelled there in his day. By Aslan's good will I was not robbed of my keys. In that tower we shall find stores of weapons and mail and some victuals also, though no better than dry biscuit. There also we can lie safe while we make our plans. And now, prithee, tell me who you two are and all your story."

"I'm Eustace Scrubb and this is Jill Pole," said the Boy. "And we were here once before, ages and ages ago, more than a year ago by our time, and there was a chap called Prince Rilian, and they were keeping this chap underground, and Puddleglum put his foot in —"

"Ha!" cried Tirian, "are you then that Eustace and that Jill who rescued King Rilian from his long enchantment?"

"Yes, that's us," said Jill. "So he's *King* Rilian now, is he? Oh of course he would be. I forgot —"

"Nay," said Tirian, "I am the seventh in descent from him. He has been dead over two hundred years."

Jill made a face. "Ugh!" she said. "That's the horrid part about coming back to Narnia." But Eustace went on.

"Well now you know who we are, Sire," he said. "And it was like this. The Professor and Aunt Polly had got all us friends of Narnia together —"

"I know not these names, Eustace," said Tirian.

"They're the two who came into Narnia at the very beginning, the day all the animals learned to talk."

"By the Lion's Mane," cried Tirian. "Those two! The Lord Digory and the Lady Polly! From the dawn of the world! And still in your place? The wonder and the glory of it! But tell me, tell me."

"She isn't really our aunt, you know," said Eustace. "She's Miss Plummer, but we call her Aunt Polly. Well those two got us all together partly just for fun, so that we could all have a good jaw about Narnia (for of course there's no one else we can ever talk to about things like that) but partly because the Professor had a feeling that we were somehow wanted over here. Well then you came in like a ghost or goodness-knows-what and nearly frightened the lives out of us and vanished without saying a word. After that, we knew for certain there was something up.

The next question was how to get here. You can't go just by wanting to. So we talked and talked and at last the Professor said the only way would be by the Magic Rings. It was by those Rings that he and Aunt Polly got here long, long ago when they were only kids, years before we younger ones were born. But the Rings had all been buried in the garden of a house in London (that's our big town, Sire) and the house had been sold. So then the problem was how to get at them. You'll never guess what we did in the end! Peter and Edmund – that's the High King Peter, the one who spoke to you – went up to London to get into the garden from the back, early in the morning before people were up. They were dressed like workmen so that if anyone did see them it would look as if they'd come to do something about the drains. I wish I'd been with them: it must have been glorious fun. And they must have succeeded for next day Peter sent us a wire – that's a sort of message, Sire, I'll explain about it some other time – to say he'd got the Rings. And the day after that was the day Pole and I had to go back to school – we're the only two who are still at school and we're at the same one. So Peter and Edmund were to meet us at a place on the way down to school and hand over the Rings. It had to be us two who were to go to Narnia, you see, because the older ones couldn't come again. So we got into the train – that's a kind of thing people travel in in our world: a lot of wagons chained together – and the Professor and Aunt Polly and Lucy came with us. We wanted to keep together as long as we could. Well there we were in the train. And we were just getting to the station where the others were to meet us, and I was looking out of the window to see if I could see them when suddenly there came a most frightful jerk and a noise: and there we

were in Narnia and there was your Majesty tied up to the tree."

"So you never used the Rings?" said Tirian.

"No," said Eustace. "Never even saw them. Aslan did it all for us in his own way without any Rings."

"But the High King Peter has them," said Tirian.

"Yes," said Jill. "But we don't think he can use them. When the two other Pevensies – King Edmund and Queen Lucy – were last here, Aslan said they would never come to Narnia again. And he said something of the same sort to the High King, only longer ago. You may be sure he'll come like a shot if he's allowed."

"Gosh!" said Eustace. "It's getting hot in this sun. Are we nearly there, Sire?"

"Look," said Tirian and pointed. Not many yards away grey battlements rose above the tree-tops, and after a minute's more walking they came out in an open grassy space. A stream ran across it and on the far side of the stream stood a squat, square tower with very few and narrow windows and one heavy-looking door in the wall that faced them.

Tirian looked sharply this way and that to make sure that no enemies were in sight. Then he walked up to the tower and stood still for a moment fishing up his bunch of keys which he wore inside his hunting-dress on a narrow silver chain that went round his neck. It was a nice bunch of keys that he brought out, for two were golden and many were richly ornamented: you could see at once that they were keys made for opening solemn and secret rooms in palaces, or chests and caskets of sweet-smelling wood that contained royal treasures. But the key which he now put into the lock of the door was big and plain and more rudely made. The lock was stiff and for a moment Tirian began to be afraid that he would not be able to turn it: but at last he did and the door swung open with a sullen creak.

"Welcome friends," said Tirian. "I fear this is the best palace that the King of Narnia can now offer to his guests."

Tirian was pleased to see that the two strangers had been well brought up. They both said not to mention it and that they were sure it would be very nice.

As a matter of fact it was not particularly nice. It was rather dark and smelled very damp. There was only one room in it and this room went right up to the stone roof: a wooden staircase in one corner led up to a trap door by which you could get out on the battlements. There were a few rude bunks to sleep in, and a great many lockers and bundles. There was also a hearth which looked as if nobody had lit a fire in it for a great many years.

"We'd better go out and gather some firewood first thing, hadn't we?" said Jill.

"Not yet, comrade," said Tirian. He was determined that they should not be caught unarmed, and began searching the lockers, thankfully remembering that he had always been careful to have these garrison towers inspected once a year and to make sure that they were stocked with all things needful. The bow strings were there in their coverings of oiled silk, the swords and spears were greased against rust, and the armour was kept bright in its wrappings. But there was something even better. "Look you!" said Tirian as he drew out a long mail shirt of a curious pattern and flashed it before the children's eyes.

"That's funny-looking mail, Sire," said Eustace.

"Aye, lad," said Tirian. "No Narnian Dwarf smithied that. 'Tis mail of Calormen, outlandish gear. I have ever kept a few suits of it in readiness, for I never knew when I or my friends might have reason to walk unseen in The Tisroc's land. And look on this stone bottle. In this there is a juice which, when we have rubbed it on our hands and faces, will make us brown as Calormenes."

"Oh hurrah!" said Jill. "Disguise! I love disguises."

Tirian showed them how to pour out a little of the juice into the palms of their hands and then rub it well over their faces and necks, right down to the shoulders, and then on their hands, right up to the elbows. He did the same himself.

"After this has hardened on us," he said, "we may wash in water and it will not change. Nothing but oil and ashes will make us white Narnians again. And now, sweet Jill, let us go see how this mail shirt becomes you. 'Tis something too long, yet not so much as I feared. Doubtless it belonged to a page in the train of one of their Tarkaans."

After the mail shirts they put on Calormene helmets, which are little round ones fitting tight to the head and having a spike on top. Then Tirian took long rolls of some white stuff out of the locker and wound them over the helmets till they became turbans: but the little steel spike still stuck up in the middle. He and Eustace took curved Calormene swords and little round shields. There was no sword light enough for Jill, but he gave her a long, straight hunting knife which might do for a sword at a pinch.

"Hast any skill with the bow, maiden?" said Tirian.

"Nothing worth talking of," said Jill, blushing. "Scrubb's not bad."

"Don't you believe her, Sire," said Eustace. "We've both been practising archery ever since we got back from Narnia last time, and she's about as good as me now. Not that either of us is much."

Then Tirian gave Jill a bow and a quiver full of arrows. The next business was to light a fire, for inside that tower it still felt more like a cave than like anything indoors and set one shivering. But they got warm gathering wood – the sun was now at its highest – and once the blaze was roaring up the chimney the place began to look cheerful. Dinner was, however, a dull meal, for the best they could do was to pound up some of the hard biscuit which they found in a locker and pour it into boiling water, with salt, so as to make a kind of porridge. And of course there was nothing to drink but water.

"I wish we'd brought a packet of tea," said Jill.

"Or a tin of cocoa," said Eustace.

"A firkin or so of good wine in each of these towers would not have been amiss," said Tirian.

CHAPTER SIX

A GOOD NIGHT'S WORK

ABOUT four hours later Tirian flung himself into one of the bunks to snatch a little sleep. The two children were already snoring: he had made them go to bed before he did because they would have to be up most of the night and he knew that at their age they couldn't do without sleep. Also, he had tired them out. First he had given Jill some practice in archery and found that, though not up to Narnian standards, she was really not too bad. Indeed she had succeeded in shooting a rabbit (not a *Talking* rabbit, of course: there are lots of the ordinary kind about in Western Narnia) and it was already skinned, cleaned, and hanging up. He had found that both the children knew all about this chilly and smelly job; they had learned that kind of thing on their great journey through Giant-Land in the days of Prince Rilian. Then he had tried to teach Eustace how to use his sword and shield. Eustace had learned quite a lot about sword fighting on his earlier adventures but that had been all with a straight Narnian sword. He had never handled a curved Calormene scimitar and that made it hard, for many of the strokes are quite different and some of the habits he had learned with the long sword had now to be unlearned again. But Tirian found that he had a good eye and was very quick on his feet. He was surprised at the strength of both children: in fact they both seemed to be already much stronger and bigger and more grown-up than they had been when he first met them a few hours ago. It is one of the effects which Narnian air often has on visitors from our world.

All three of them agreed that the very first thing they

must do was to go back to Stable Hill and try to rescue Jewel the Unicorn. After that, if they succeeded, they would try to get away Eastward and meet the little army which Roonwit the Centaur would be bringing from Cair Paravel.

An experienced warrior and huntsman like Tirian can always wake up at the time he wants. So he gave himself till nine o'clock that night and then put all worries out of his head and fell asleep at once. It seemed only a moment later when he woke but he knew by the light and the very feel of things that he had timed his sleep exactly. He got up, put on his helmet-and-turban (he had slept in his mail shirt), and then shook the other two till they woke up. They looked, to tell the truth, very grey and dismal as they climbed out of their bunks and there was a good deal of yawning.

"Now," said Tirian, "we go due North from here – by good fortune 'tis a starry night – and it will be much shorter than our journey this morning, for then we went round-about but now we shall go straight. If we are challenged, then do you two hold your peace and I will do my best to talk like a curst, cruel, proud lord of Calormen. If I draw my sword then thou, Eustace, must do likewise and let Jill leap behind us and stand with an arrow on the string. But if I cry 'Home', then fly for the Tower both of you. And let none try to fight on – not even one stroke – after I have given the retreat: such false valour has spoiled many notable plans in the wars. And now, friends, in the name of Aslan let us go forward."

Out they went into the cold night. All the great Northern stars were burning above the tree-tops. The North-Star of that world is called the Spear-Head: it is brighter than our Pole Star.

For a time they could go straight towards the Spear-Head but presently they came to a dense thicket so that they had to go out of their course to get round it. And after that – for they were still overshadowed by branches – it was hard to pick up their bearings. It was Jill who set them right again: she had been an excellent Guide in England. And of course she knew her Narnian stars perfectly, having travelled so much in the wild Northern Lands, and could work out the direction from other stars even when the Spear-Head was hidden. As soon as Tirian saw that she was the best pathfinder of the three of them he put her in front. And then he was astonished to find how silently and almost invisibly she glided on before them.

"By the Mane!" he whispered to Eustace. "This girl is a wondrous wood-maid. If she had Dryad's blood in her she could scarce do it better."

"She's so small, that's what helps," whispered Eustace. But Jill from in front said: "S-s-s-h, less noise."

All round them the wood was very quiet. Indeed it was far too quiet. On an ordinary Narnia night there ought to have been noises – an occasional cheery "Goodnight" from a Hedgehog, the cry of an Owl overhead, perhaps a flute in the distance to tell of Fauns dancing, or some throbbing, hammering noises from Dwarfs underground. All that was silenced: gloom and fear reigned over Narnia.

After a time they began to go steeply uphill and the trees grew further apart. Tirian could dimly make out the well-known hill-top and the stable. Jill was now going with more and more caution: she kept on making signs to the others with her hand to do the same. Then she stopped dead still and Tirian saw her gradually sink down into the grass and disappear without a sound. A moment later she rose again, put her mouth close to Tirian's ear, and said in the lowest possible whisper, "Get down. *Thee* better." She said *thee* for *see* not because she had a lisp but because she knew the hissing letter S is the part of a whisper most likely to be overheard. Tirian at once lay down, almost as silently as Jill, but not quite, for he was heavier and older. And once they were down, he saw how from that position you could see the edge of the hill sharp against the star-strewn sky. Two black shapes rose against it: one was the stable, and the other, a few feet in front of it, was a Calormene sentry. He was keeping very ill watch: not walking or even standing but sitting with his spear over his shoulder and his chin on his chest. "Well done," said Tirian to Jill. She had shown him exactly what he needed to know.

They got up and Tirian now took the lead. Very slowly, hardly daring to breathe, they made their way up to a little clump of trees which was not more than forty feet away from the sentinel.

"Wait here till I come again," he whispered to the other two. "If I miscarry, fly." Then he sauntered out boldly in full view of the enemy. The man started when he saw him

and was just going to jump to his feet: he was afraid Tirian might be one of his own officers and that he would get into trouble for sitting down. But before he could get up Tirian had dropped on one knee beside him, saying:

"Art thou a warrior of the Tisroc's, may he live for ever? It cheers my heart to meet thee among all these beasts and devils of Narnians. Give me thy hand, friend."

Before he well knew what was happening the Calormene sentry found his right hand seized in a mighty grip. Next instant someone was kneeling on his legs and a dagger was pressed against his neck.

"One noise and thou art dead," said Tirian in his ear. "Tell me where the Unicorn is and thou shalt live."

"B – behind the stable, O My Master," stammered the unfortunate man.

"Good. Rise up and lead me to him."

As the man got up the point of the dagger never left his neck. It only travelled round (cold and rather ticklish) as Tirian got behind him and settled it at a convenient place under his ear. Trembling he went round to the back of the stable.

Though it was dark Tirian could see the white shape of Jewel at once.

"Hush!" he said. "No, do not neigh. Yes, Jewel, it is I. How have they tied thee?"

"Hobbled by all four legs and tied with a bridle to a ring in the stable wall," came Jewel's voice.

"Stand here, sentry, with your back to the wall. So. Now, Jewel: set the point of your horn against this Calormene's breast."

"With a good will, Sire," said Jewel.

"If he moves, rive him to the heart." Then in a few seconds Tirian cut the ropes. With the remains of them he bound the sentry hand and foot. Finally he made him open his mouth, stuffed it full of grass and tied him up from scalp to chin so that he could make no noise, lowered the man into a sitting position and set him against the wall.

"I have done thee some discourtesy, soldier," said Tirian. "But such was my need. If we meet again I may happen to do thee a better turn. Now, Jewel, let us go softly."

He put his left arm round the beast's neck and bent and kissed its nose and both had great joy. They went back as quietly as possible to the place where he had left the children. It was darker in there under the trees and he nearly ran into Eustace before he saw him.

"All's well," whispered Tirian. "A good night's work. Now for home."

They turned and had gone a few paces when Eustace said, "Where are you, Pole?" There was no answer. "Is Jill on the other side of you, Sire?" he asked.

"What?" said Tirian. "Is she not on the other side of you?"

It was a terrible moment. They dared not shout but they whispered her name in the loudest whisper they could manage. There was no reply.

"Did she go from you while I was away?" asked Tirian.

"I didn't see or hear her go," said Eustace. "But she could have gone without my knowing. She can be as quiet as a cat; you've seen for yourself."

At that moment a far off drum beat was heard. Jewel moved his ears forward. "Dwarfs," he said.

"And treacherous Dwarfs, enemies, as likely as not," muttered Tirian.

"And here comes something on hoofs, much nearer," said Jewel.

The two humans and the Unicorn stood dead still. There were now so many different things to worry about that they didn't know what to do. The noise of hoofs came steadily nearer. And then, quite close to them, a voice whispered:

"Hallo! Are you all there?"

Thank heaven, it was Jill's.

"Where the *devil* have you been to?" said Eustace in a furious whisper, for he had been very frightened.

"In the stable," gasped Jill, but it was the sort of gasp you give when you're struggling with suppressed laughter.

"Oh," growled Eustace, "you think it funny, do you? Well all I can say is –"

"Have you got Jewel, Sire?" asked Jill.

"Yes. Here he is. What is that beast with you?"

"That's *him*," said Jill. "But let's be off home before anyone wakes up." And again there came little explosions of laughter.

The others obeyed at once for they had already lingered long enough in that dangerous place and the Dwarf drums seemed to have come a little nearer. It was only after they had been walking Southward for several minutes that Eustace said:

"Got *him*? What do you mean?"

"The false Aslan," said Jill.

"What?" said Tirian. "Where have you been? What have you done?"

"Well, Sire," said Jill. "As soon as I saw that you'd got the sentry out of the way I thought hadn't I better have a look inside the stable and see what really *is* there? So I crawled along. It was as easy as anything to draw the bolt.

Of course it was pitch black inside and smelled like any other stable. Then I struck a light and – would you believe it? – there was nothing at all there but this old donkey with a bundle of lion-skin tied on to his back. So I drew my knife and told him he'd have to come along with me. As a matter of fact I needn't have threatened him with the knife at all. He was very fed up with the stable and quite ready to come – weren't you, Puzzle dear?"

"Great Scott!" said Eustace. "Well I'm – jiggered. I was jolly angry with you a moment ago, and I still think it was mean of you to sneak off without the rest of us: but I must admit – well, I mean to say – well it was a perfectly gorgeous thing to do. If she was a boy she'd have to be knighted, wouldn't she, Sire?"

"If she was a boy," said Tirian, "she'd be whipped for disobeying orders." And in the dark no one could see whether he said this with a frown or a smile. Next minute there was a sound of rasping metal.

"What are you doing, Sire?" asked Jewel sharply.

"Drawing my sword to smite off the head of the accursed Ass," said Tirian in a terrible voice. "Stand clear, girl."

"Oh don't, please don't," said Jill. "Really, you mustn't. It wasn't his fault. It was all the Ape. He didn't know any better. And he's very sorry. And he's a nice Donkey. His name's Puzzle. And I've got my arms round his neck."

"Jill," said Tirian, "you are the bravest and most wood-wise of all my subjects, but also the most malapert and disobedient. Well: let the Ass live. What have you to say for yourself, Ass?"

"Me, Sire?" came the Donkey's voice. "I'm sure I'm very sorry if I've done wrong. The Ape said Aslan *wanted* me to dress up like that. And I thought he'd know. I'm not clever like him. I only did what I was told. It wasn't any fun for me living in that stable. I don't even know what's been going on outside. He never let me out except for a minute or two at night. Some days they forgot to give me any water too."

"Sire," said Jewel. "Those Dwarfs are coming nearer and nearer. Do we want to meet them?"

Tirian thought for a moment and then suddenly gave a great laugh out loud. Then he spoke, not this time in a whisper. "By the Lion," he said, "I am growing slow witted! Meet them? Certainly we will meet them. We will meet anyone now. We have this Ass to show them. Let them see the thing they have feared and bowed to. We can show them the truth of the Ape's vile plot. His secret's out. The tide's turned. Tomorrow we shall hang that Ape on the highest tree in Narnia. No more whispering and skulking and disguises. Where are these honest Dwarfs? We have good news for them."

When you have been whispering for hours the mere sound of anyone talking out loud has a wonderfully stirring effect. The whole party began talking and laughing: even Puzzle lifted up his head and gave a grand Haw-hee-haw-hee-hee; a thing the Ape hadn't allowed him

to do for days. Then they set off in the direction of the drumming. It grew steadily louder and soon they could see torchlight as well. They came out on one of those rough roads (we should hardly call them roads at all in England) which ran through Lantern Waste. And there, marching sturdily along, were about thirty Dwarfs, all with their little spades and mattocks over their shoulders. Two armed Calormenes led the column and two more brought up the rear.

"Stay!" thundered Tirian as he stepped out on the road. "Stay, soldiers. Whither do you lead these Narnian Dwarfs and by whose orders?"

CHAPTER SEVEN

MAINLY ABOUT DWARFS

THE two Calormene soldiers at the head of the column, seeing what they took for a Tarkaan or great lord with two armed pages, came to a halt and raised their spears in salute.

"O My Master," said one of them, "we lead these manikins to Calormen to work in the mines of The Tisroc, may-he-live-forever."

"By the great god Tash, they are very obedient," said Tirian. Then suddenly he turned to the Dwarfs themselves. About one in six of them carried a torch and by that flickering light he could see their bearded faces all looking at him with grim and dogged expressions. "Has The Tisroc fought a great battle, Dwarfs, and conquered your land?" he asked, "that thus you go patiently to die in the salt-pits of Pugrahan?"

The two soldiers glared at him in surprise but the Dwarfs all answered, "Aslan's orders, Aslan's orders. He's sold us. What can we do against *him*?"

"Tisroc indeed!" added one and spat. "I'd like to see him try it!"

"Silence, dogs!" said the chief soldier.

"Look!" said Tirian, pulling Puzzle forward into the light. "It has all been a lie. Aslan has not come to Narnia at all. You have been cheated by the Ape. This is the thing he brought out of the stable to show you. Look at it."

What the Dwarfs saw, now that they could see it close, was certainly enough to make them wonder how they had ever been taken in. The lion-skin had got pretty untidy already during Puzzle's imprisonment in the stable and it had been knocked crooked during his journey through the dark wood. Most of it was in a big lump on one shoulder. The head, besides being pushed sideways, had somehow got very far back so that anyone could now see his silly, gentle, donkeyish face gazing out of it. Some grass stuck out of one corner of his mouth, for he'd been doing a little

quiet nibbling as they brought him along. And he was muttering, "It wasn't my fault, I'm not clever. I never said I *was*."

For one second all the Dwarfs were staring at Puzzle with wide open mouths and then one of the soldiers said sharply, "Are you mad, My Master? What are you doing to the slaves?" and the other said, "And who are you?" Neither of their spears was at the salute now – both were down and ready for action.

"Give the password," said the chief soldier.

"This is my password," said the King as he drew his sword. "*The light is dawning, the lie broken.* Now guard thee, miscreant, for I am Tirian of Narnia."

He flew upon the chief soldier like lightning. Eustace, who had drawn his sword when he saw the King draw his, rushed at the other one: his face was deadly pale, but I wouldn't blame him for that. And he had the luck that beginners sometimes do have. He forgot all that Tirian had tried to teach him that afternoon, slashed wildly (indeed I'm not sure his eyes weren't shut) and suddenly found, to his own great surprise, that the Calormene lay dead at his feet. And though that was a great relief, it was, at the moment, rather frightening. The King's fight lasted a second or two longer: then he too had killed his man and shouted to Eustace, "'Ware the other two."

But the Dwarfs had settled the two remaining Calormenes. There was no enemy left.

"Well struck, Eustace!" cried Tirian, clapping him on the back. "Now, Dwarfs, you are free. Tomorrow I will lead you to free all Narnia. Three cheers for Aslan!"

But the result which followed was simply wretched. There was a feeble attempt from a few Dwarfs (about five) which died away all at once: from several others there were sulky growls. Many said nothing at all.

"Don't they understand?" said Jill impatiently. "What's wrong with all you Dwarfs? Don't you hear what the King says? It's all over. The Ape isn't going to rule Narnia any longer. Everyone can go back to ordinary life. You can have fun again. Aren't you glad?"

After a pause of nearly a minute a not-very-nice-looking Dwarf with hair and beard as black as soot said: "And who might you be, Missie?"

"I'm Jill," she said. "The same Jill who rescued King

Rilian from the enchantment —
and this is Eustace who did it too
— and we've come back from
another world after hundreds of
years. Aslan sent us."

The Dwarfs all looked at one
another with grins; sneering
grins, not merry ones.

"Well," said the Black Dwarf
(whose name was Griffle), "I
don't know how all you chaps
feel, but I feel I've heard as much
about Aslan as I want to for the
rest of my life."

"That's right, that's right," growled the other Dwarfs.
"It's all a plant, all a blooming plant."

"What do you mean?" said Tirian. He had not been pale
when he was fighting but he was pale now. He had thought
this was going to be a beautiful moment, but it was turning
out more like a bad dream.

"You must think we're blooming soft in the head, that
you must," said Griffle. "We've been taken in once and
now you expect us to be taken in again the next minute.
We've no more use for stories about Aslan, see! Look at
him! An old moke with long ears!"

"By heaven, you make me mad," said Tirian. "Which
of us said *that* was Aslan? That is the Ape's imitation of the real Aslan. Can't you understand?"

"And you've got a better imitation, I suppose!" said
Griffle. "No thanks. We've been fooled once and we're not
going to be fooled again."

"I have not," said Tirian angrily, "I serve the real
Aslan."

"Where's he? Who's he? Show him to us!" said several Dwarfs.

"Do you think I keep him in my wallet, fools?" said Tirian. "Who am I that I could make Aslan appear at my bidding? He's not a tame lion."

The moment those words were out of his mouth he realized that he had made a false move. The Dwarfs at once began repeating "not a tame lion, not a tame lion," in a jeering sing-song. "That's what the other lot kept on telling us," said one.

"Do you mean you don't believe in the real Aslan?" said Jill. "But I've seen him. And he has sent us two here out of a different world."

"Ah," said Griffle with a broad smile. "So *you* say. They've taught you your stuff all right. Saying your lessons, ain't you?"

"Churl," cried Tirian, "will you give a lady the lie to her very face?"

"You keep a civil tongue in your head, Mister," replied the Dwarf. "I don't think we want any more Kings – if you *are* Tirian, which you don't look like him – no more than we want any Aslans. We're going to look after ourselves from now on and touch our caps to nobody. See?"

"That's right," said the other Dwarfs. "We're on our own now. No more Aslan, no more Kings, no more silly stories about other worlds. The Dwarfs are for the Dwarfs." And they began to fall into their places and to get ready for marching back to wherever they had come from.

"Little beasts!" said Eustace. "Aren't you even going to say *thank you* for being saved from the salt-mines?"

"Oh, we know all about that," said Griffle over his shoulder. "You wanted to make use of us, that's why you rescued us. You're playing some game of your own. Come on you chaps."

And the Dwarfs struck up the queer little marching song which goes with the drum-beat, and off they tramped into the darkness.

Tirian and his friends stared after them. Then he said the single word "Come," and they continued their journey.

They were a silent party. Puzzle felt himself to be still in disgrace, and also he didn't really quite understand what had happened. Jill, besides being disgusted with the Dwarfs, was very impressed with Eustace's victory over the Calormene and felt almost shy. As for Eustace, his heart was still beating rather quickly. Tirian and Jewel walked sadly together in the rear. The King had his arm on the Unicorn's shoulder and sometimes the Unicorn nuzzled the King's cheek with his soft nose. They did not try to comfort one another with words. It wasn't very easy to think of anything to say that would be comforting. Tirian had never dreamed that one of the results of an Ape's setting up as a false Aslan would be to stop people from believing in the real one. He had felt quite sure that the Dwarfs would rally to his side the moment he showed them how they had been deceived. And then next night he would have led them to Stable Hill and shown Puzzle to all the creatures and everyone would have turned against the Ape and, perhaps after a scuffle with the Calormenes, the whole thing would have been over. But now, it seemed, he could count on nothing. How many other Narnians might turn the same way as the Dwarfs?

"Somebody's coming after us, I think," said Puzzle suddenly.

They stopped and listened. Sure enough, there was a thump-thump of small feet behind them.

"Who goes there!" shouted the King.

"Only me, Sire," came a voice. "Me, Poggin the Dwarf. I've only just managed to get away from the others. I'm on your side, Sire: and on Aslan's. If you can put a Dwarfish sword in my fist, I'd gladly strike a blow on the right side before all's done."

Everyone crowded round him and welcomed him and praised him and slapped him on the back. Of course one single Dwarf could not make a very great difference, but it was somehow very cheering to have even one. The whole party brightened up. But Jill and Eustace didn't stay bright for very long, for they were now yawning their heads off

and too tired to think about anything but bed.

It was at the coldest hour of the night, just before dawn, that they got back to the Tower. If there had been a meal ready for them they would have been glad enough to eat, but the bother and delay of getting one was not to be thought of. They drank from a stream, splashed their faces with water, and tumbled into

their bunks, except for Puzzle and Jewel who said they'd be more comfortable outside. This perhaps was just as well, for a Unicorn and a fat, full-grown Donkey indoors always make a room feel rather crowded.

Narnian Dwarfs, though less than four feet high, are for their size about the toughest and strongest creatures there are, so that Poggin, in spite of a heavy day and a late night, woke fully refreshed before any of the others. He at once took Jill's bow, went out and shot a couple of wood pigeons. Then he sat plucking them on the doorstep and

chatting to Jewel and Puzzle. Puzzle looked and felt a good
deal better this morning. Jewel, being a Unicorn and therefore one of the noblest and delicatest of beasts, had been
very kind to him, talking to him about things of the sort
they could both understand like grass and sugar and the
care of one's hoofs. When Jill and Eustace came out of the
Tower yawning and rubbing their eyes at almost half past
ten, the Dwarf showed them where they could gather
plenty of a Narnian weed called Wild Fresney, which looks
rather like our wood-sorrel but tastes a good deal nicer
when cooked. (It needs a little butter and pepper to make it
perfect, but they hadn't got these.) So that what with one
thing and another, they had the makings of a capital stew
for their breakfast or dinner, whichever you choose to call
it. Tirian went a little further off into the wood with an axe
and brought back some branches for fuel. While the meal
was cooking – which seemed a very long time, especially
as it smelled nicer and nicer the nearer it came to being
done – the King found a complete Dwarfish outfit for
Poggin: mail shirt, helmet, shield, sword, belt, and dagger.
Then he inspected Eustace's sword and found that Eustace
had put it back in the sheath all messy from killing the
Calormene. He was scolded for that and made to clean and
polish it.

All this while Jill went to and fro, sometimes stirring the
pot and sometimes looking out enviously at the Donkey
and the Unicorn who were contentedly grazing. How many
times that morning she wished she could eat grass!

But when the meal came everyone felt it had been worth
waiting for, and there were second helpings all round.
When everyone had eaten as much as he could, the three
humans and the Dwarf came and sat on the doorstep, the
four-footed ones lay down facing them, the Dwarf (with

permission both from Jill and from Tirian) lit his pipe, and the King said:

"Now, friend Poggin, you have more news of the enemy, belike, than we. Tell us all you know. And first, what tale do they tell of my escape?"

"As cunning a tale, Sire, as ever was devised," said Poggin. "It was the Cat, Ginger, who told it, and most likely made it up too. This Ginger, Sire – oh, he's a slyboots if ever a cat was – said he was walking past the tree to which those villains bound your Majesty. And he said (saving your reverence) that you were howling and swearing and cursing Aslan: 'language I wouldn't like to repeat' were the words he used, looking ever so prim and proper – you know the way a Cat can when it pleases. And then, says Ginger, Aslan himself suddenly appeared in a flash of lightning and swallowed your Majesty up at one mouthful. All the Beasts trembled at this story and some fainted right away. And of course the Ape followed it up. There, he says, see what Aslan does to those who don't respect him. Let that be a warning to you all. And the poor creatures wailed and whined and said, it will, it will. So that in the upshot your Majesty's escape has not set them thinking whether you still have loyal friends to aid you, but only made them more afraid and more obedient to the Ape."

"What devilish policy!" said Tirian. "This Ginger, then, is close in the Ape's counsels."

"It's more a question by now, Sire, if the Ape is in *his* counsels," replied the Dwarf. "The Ape has taken to drinking, you see. My belief is that the plot is now mostly carried on by Ginger or Rishda – that's the Calormene captain. And I think some words that Ginger has scattered among the Dwarfs are chiefly to blame for the scurvy return they made you. And I'll tell you why. One of those dreadful midnight meetings had just broken up the night before last and I'd gone a bit of the way home when I found I'd left my pipe behind. It was a real good 'un, an old favourite, so I went back to look for it. But before I got to the place where I'd been sitting (it was black as pitch there) I heard a cat's voice say *Mew* and a Calormene voice say 'here . . . speak softly,' so I just stood as still as if I was frozen. And these two were Ginger and Rishda Tarkaan as they call him. 'Noble Tarkaan,' said the Cat in that silky voice of his, 'I just wanted to know exactly what we both meant today about Aslan meaning *no more* than Tash.' 'Doubtless, most sagacious of cats,' says the other, 'you have perceived my meaning.' 'You mean,' says Ginger, 'that there's no such person as either.' 'All who are enlightened know that,' said the Tarkaan. 'Then we can understand one another,' purrs the Cat. 'Do you, like me, grow a little weary of the Ape?' 'A stupid, greedy brute,' says the other, 'but we must use him for the present. Thou and I must provide for all things in secret and make the Ape do our will.' 'And it would be better, wouldn't it,' said Ginger, 'to let some of the more enlightened Narnians into our counsels: one by one as we find them apt. For the Beasts who really believe in Aslan may turn at any moment: and will, if the Ape's folly betrays his secret. But those who care neither for Tash nor Aslan but have only an eye to their own profit and such reward as The Tisroc may give them when Narnia is a Calormene province, will be firm.' 'Excellent Cat,' said the Captain. 'But choose which ones carefully.'"

While the Dwarf had been speaking the day seemed to have changed. It had been sunny when they sat down. Now Puzzle shivered. Jewel shifted his head uneasily. Jill looked up.

"It's clouding over," she said.

"And it's so cold," said Puzzle.

"Cold enough, by the Lion!" said Tirian, blowing on his hands. "And faugh! What foul smell is this?"

"Phew!" gasped Eustace. "It's like something dead. Is there a dead bird somewhere about? And why didn't we notice it before?"

With a great upheaval Jewel scrambled to his feet and pointed with his horn.

"Look!" he cried. "Look at it! Look, look!"

Then all six of them saw; and over all their faces there came an expression of uttermost dismay.

CHAPTER EIGHT

WHAT NEWS THE EAGLE BROUGHT

In the shadow of the trees on the far side of the clearing something was moving. It was gliding very slowly Northward. At a first glance you might have mistaken it for smoke, for it was grey and you could see things through it. But the deathly smell was not the smell of smoke. Also, this thing kept its shape instead of billowing and curling as smoke would have done. It was roughly the shape of a man but it had the head of a bird; some bird of prey with a cruel, curved beak. It had four arms which it held high above its head, stretching them out Northward as if it wanted to snatch all Narnia in its grip; and its fingers – all twenty of them – were curved like its beak and had long, pointed, bird-like claws instead of nails. It floated on the grass instead of walking, and the grass seemed to wither beneath it.

After one look at it Puzzle gave a screaming bray and darted into the Tower. And Jill (who was no coward, as you know) hid her face in her hands to shut out the sight of it. The others watched it for perhaps a minute, until it streamed away into the thicker trees on their right and disappeared. Then the sun came out again, and the birds once more began to sing.

Everyone started breathing properly again and moved. They had all been still as statues while it was in sight.

"What was it?" said Eustace in a whisper.

"I have seen it once before," said Tirian. "But that time it was carved in stone and overlaid with gold and had solid diamonds for eyes. It was when I was no older than thou, and had gone as a guest to The Tisroc's court in Tashbaan.

He took me into the great temple of Tash. There I saw it, carved above the altar."

"Then that – that thing – was Tash?" said Eustace.

But instead of answering him Tirian slipped his arm behind Jill's shoulders and said, "How is it with you, Lady?"

"A-all right," said Jill, taking her hands away from her pale face and trying to smile. "I'm all right. It only made me feel a little sick for a moment."

"It seems, then," said the Unicorn, "that there is a real Tash, after all."

"Yes," said the Dwarf. "And this fool of an Ape, who didn't believe in Tash, will get more than he bargained for! He called for Tash: Tash has come."

"Where has it – he – the Thing – gone to?" said Jill.

"North into the heart of Narnia," said Tirian. "It has

come to dwell among us. They have called it and it has come."

"Ho, ho, ho!" chuckled the Dwarf, rubbing his hairy hands together. "It will be a surprise for the Ape. People shouldn't call for demons unless they really mean what they say."

"Who knows if Tash will be visible to the Ape?" said Jewel.

"Where has Puzzle got to?" said Eustace.

They all shouted out Puzzle's name and Jill went round to the other side of the Tower to see if he had gone there.

They were quite tired of looking for him when at last his large grey head peered cautiously out of the doorway and he said, "Has it gone away?" And when at last they got him to come out, he was shivering the way a dog shivers before a thunderstorm.

"I see now," said Puzzle, "that I really have been a very bad donkey. I ought never to have listened to Shift. I never thought things like this would begin to happen."

"If you'd spent less time saying you weren't clever and more time trying to be as clever as you could —" began Eustace but Jill interrupted him.

"Oh leave poor old Puzzle alone," she said. "It was all a mistake; wasn't it, Puzzle dear?" And she kissed him on the nose.

Though rather shaken by what they had seen, the whole party now sat down again and went on with their talk.

Jewel had little to tell them. While he was a prisoner he had spent nearly all his time tied up at the back of the stable, and had of course heard none of the enemies' plans. He had been kicked (he'd done some kicking back too) and beaten and threatened with death unless he would say that he believed it was Aslan who was brought out and shown to them by firelight every night. In fact he was going to be executed this very morning if he had not been rescued. He didn't know what had happened to the Lamb.

The question they had to decide was whether they would go to Stable Hill again that night, show Puzzle to the Narnians and try to make them see how they had been tricked, or whether they should steal away Eastward to meet the help which Roonwit the Centaur was bringing up from Cair Paravel and return against the Ape and his Calormenes in force. Tirian would very much like to have followed the first plan: he hated the idea of leaving the Ape to bully his people one moment longer than need be. On the other hand, the way the Dwarfs had behaved last night was a warning. Apparently one couldn't be sure how people would take it even if he showed them Puzzle. And there were the Calormene soldiers to be reckoned with. Poggin thought there were about thirty of them. Tirian felt sure that if the Narnians all rallied to his side, he and Jewel and the children and Poggin (Puzzle didn't count for much) would have a good chance of beating them. But how if half the Narnians – including all the Dwarfs – just sat and looked on? or even fought against him? The risk was too great. And there was, too, the cloudy shape of Tash. What might it do?

And then, as Poggin pointed out, there was no harm in leaving the Ape to deal with his own difficulties for a day or two. He would have no Puzzle to bring out and show now. It wasn't easy to see what story he – or Ginger – could make up to explain that. If the Beasts asked night after night to see Aslan, and no Aslan was brought out, surely even the simplest of them would get suspicious.

In the end they all agreed that the best thing was to go off and try to meet Roonwit.

As soon as they had decided this, it was wonderful how much more cheerful everyone became. I don't honestly think that this was because any of them was afraid of a fight (except perhaps Jill and Eustace). But I daresay that each of them, deep down inside, was very glad not to go any nearer – or not yet – to that horrible bird-headed thing which, visible or invisible, was now probably haunting Stable Hill. Anyway, one always feels better when one has made up one's mind.

Tirian said they had better remove their disguises, as they didn't want to be mistaken for Calormenes and perhaps attacked by any loyal Narnians they might meet. The Dwarf made up a horrid-looking mess of ashes from the hearth and grease out of the jar of grease which was kept for rubbing on swords and spear-heads. Then they took off their Calormene armour and went down to the stream. The nasty mixture made a lather just like soft soap: it was a pleasant, homely sight to see Tirian and the two children kneeling beside the water and scrubbing the backs of their necks or puffing and blowing as they splashed the lather off. Then they went back to the Tower with red, shiny faces, like people who have been given an extra good wash before a party. They re-armed themselves in true Narnian style, with straight swords and three-cornered shields. "Body of me," said Tirian. "That is better. I feel a true man again."

Puzzle begged very hard to have the lion-skin taken off him. He said it was too hot and the way it was rucked up on his back was uncomfortable: also, it made him look so silly. But they told him he would have to wear it a bit longer, for they still wanted to show him in that get-up to the other Beasts, even though they were now going to meet Roonwit first.

What was left of the pigeon-meat and rabbit-meat was not worth bringing away but they took some biscuits. Then Tirian locked the door of the Tower and that was the end of their stay there.

It was a little after two in the afternoon when they set out, and it was the first really warm day of that spring. The young leaves seemed to be much further out than yesterday: the snow-drops were over, but they saw several primroses. The sunlight slanted through the trees, birds sang, and always (though usually out of sight) there was the noise of running water. It was hard to think of horrible things like Tash. The children felt, "This is really Narnia at last." Even Tirian's heart grew lighter as he walked ahead of them, humming an old Narnian marching song which had the refrain:

> Ho, rumble, rumble, rumble,
> Rumble drum belaboured.

After the King came Eustace and Poggin the Dwarf. Poggin was telling Eustace the names of all the Narnian trees, birds, and plants which he didn't know already. Sometimes Eustace would tell him about English ones.

After them came Puzzle, and after him Jill and Jewel walking very close together. Jill had, as you might say, quite fallen in love with the Unicorn. She thought — and she wasn't far wrong — that he was the shiningest, delicatest, most graceful animal she had ever met: and he was so gentle and soft of speech that, if you hadn't known, you would hardly have believed how fierce and terrible he could be in battle.

"Oh, this *is* nice!" said Jill. "Just walking along like this. I wish there could be more of *this* sort of adventure. It's a pity there's always so much happening in Narnia."

But the Unicorn explained to her that she was quite mistaken. He said that the Sons and Daughters of Adam and Eve were brought out of their own strange world into Narnia only at times when Narnia was stirred and upset, but she mustn't think it was always like that. In between their visits there were hundreds and thousands of years when peaceful King followed peaceful King till you could hardly remember their names or count their numbers, and there was really hardly anything to put into the History Books. And he went on to talk of old Queens and heroes whom she had never heard of. He spoke of Swanwhite the Queen who had lived before the days of the White Witch and the Great Winter, who was so beautiful that when she looked into any forest pool the reflection of her face shone out of the water like a star by night for a year and a day afterwards. He spoke of Moonwood the Hare who had such ears that he could sit by Caldron Pool under the thunder of the great waterfall and hear what men spoke in whispers at Cair Paravel. He told how King Gale, who was ninth in descent from Frank the first of all Kings, had sailed far away into the Eastern seas and delivered the Lone Islanders from a dragon and how, in return, they had given him the Lone Islands to be part of the royal lands of Narnia for ever. He talked of whole centuries in which all Narnia was so happy that notable dances and feasts, or at most tournaments, were the only things that could be remembered, and every day and week had been better than the last. And as he went on, the picture of all those happy years, all the thousands of them, piled up in Jill's mind till it was rather like looking down from a high hill on to a rich, lovely plain full of woods and waters and cornfields, which spread away and away till it got thin and misty from distance. And she said:

"Oh, I do hope we can soon settle the Ape and get back to those good, ordinary times. And then I hope they'll go on for ever and ever and ever. *Our* world is going to have an end some day. Perhaps this one won't. Oh Jewel – wouldn't it be lovely if Narnia just went on and on – like what you said it has been?"

"Nay, sister," answered Jewel, "all worlds draw to an end, except Aslan's own country."

"Well, at least," said Jill, "I hope the end of this one is millions of millions of millions of years away – hallo! what are we stopping for?"

The King and Eustace and the Dwarf were all staring up at the sky. Jill shuddered, remembering what horrors they had seen already. But it was nothing of that sort this time. It was small, and looked black against the blue.

"I dare swear," said the Unicorn, "from its flight, that it is a Talking bird."

"So think I," said the King. "But is it a friend, or a spy of the Ape's?"

"To me, Sire," said the Dwarf, "it has a look of Far-sight the Eagle."

"Ought we to hide under the trees?" said Eustace.

"Nay," said Tirian, "best stand still as rocks. He would see us for certain if we moved."

"Look! He wheels, he has seen us already," said Jewel. "He is coming down in wide circles."

"Arrow on string, Lady," said Tirian to Jill. "But by no means shoot till I bid you. He may be a friend."

If one had known what was going to happen next it would have been a treat to watch the grace and ease with which the huge bird glided down. He alighted on a rocky crag a few feet from Tirian, bowed his crested head, and said in his strange eagle's-voice, "Hail, King."

"Hail, Farsight," said Tirian. "And since you call mè King, I may well believe you are not a follower of the Ape and his false Aslan. I am right glad of your coming."

"Sire," said the Eagle, "when you have heard my news you will be sorrier of my coming than of the greatest woe that ever befell you."

Tirian's heart seemed to stop beating at these words, but he set his teeth and said, "Tell on."

"Two sights have I seen," said Farsight. "One was Cair Paravel filled with dead Narnians and living Calormenes: The Tisroc's banner advanced upon your royal battlements: and your subjects flying from the city – this way and that, into the woods. Cair Paravel was taken from the sea. Twenty great ships of Calormen put in there in the dark of the night before last night."

No one could speak.

"And the other sight, five leagues nearer than Cair Paravel, was Roonwit the Centaur lying dead with a Calormene arrow in his side. I was with him in his last hour and he gave me this message to your Majesty: to remember that all worlds draw to an end and that noble death is a treasure which no one is too poor to buy."

"So," said the King, after a long silence, "Narnia is no more."

CHAPTER NINE

THE GREAT MEETING ON STABLE HILL

FOR a long time they could not speak nor even shed a tear. Then the Unicorn stamped the ground with his hoof, and shook his mane, and spoke.

"Sire," he said, "there is now no need of counsel. We see that the Ape's plans were laid deeper than we dreamed of. Doubtless he has been long in secret traffic with The Tisroc, and as soon as he had found the lion-skin he sent him word to make ready his navy for the taking of Cair Paravel and all Narnia. Nothing now remains for us seven but to go back to Stable Hill, proclaim the truth, and take the adventure that Aslan sends us. And if, by a great marvel, we defeat those thirty Calormenes who are with the Ape, then to turn again and die in battle with the far greater host of them that will soon march from Cair Paravel."

Tirian nodded. But he turned to the children and said: "Now, friends, it is time for you to go hence into your own world. Doubtless you have done all that you were sent to do."

"B – but we've done nothing," said Jill who was shivering, not with fear exactly but because everything was so horrible.

"Nay," said the King, "you loosed me from the tree: you glided before me like a snake last night in the wood and took Puzzle: and you, Eustace, killed your man. But you are too young to share in such a bloody end as we others must meet tonight or, it may be, three days hence. I entreat you – nay, I command you – to return to your own place. I should be put to shame if I let such young warriors fall in battle on my side."

"No, no, no," said Jill (very white when she began speaking and then suddenly very red and then white again.) "We won't, I don't care what you say. We're going to stick to you whatever happens, aren't we, Eustace?"

"Yes, but there's no need to get so worked up about it," said Eustace who had stuck his hands in his pockets (forgetting how very odd that looks when you are wearing a mail shirt). "Because, you see, we haven't any choice. What's the good of talking about our going back! How? We've got no magic for doing it!"

This was very good sense but, at the moment, Jill hated Eustace for saying it. He was fond of being dreadfully matter-of-fact when other people got excited.

When Tirian realized that the two strangers could not get home (unless Aslan suddenly whisked them away), he next wanted them to go across the Southern mountains into Archenland where they might possibly be safe. But they didn't know their way and there was no one to send with them. Also, as Poggin said, once the Calormenes had Narnia they would certainly take Archenland in the next week or so: The Tisroc had always wanted to have these Northern countries for his own. In the end Eustace and Jill begged so hard that Tirian said they could come with him and take their chance – or, as he much more sensibly called it, "the adventure that Aslan would send them".

The King's first idea was that they should not go back to Stable Hill – they were sick of the very name of it by now – till after dark. But the Dwarf told them that if they arrived there by daylight they would probably find the place deserted, except perhaps for a Calormene sentry. The Beasts were far too frightened by what the Ape (and Ginger) had told them about this new angry Aslan – or Tashlan – to go near it except when they were called together for these horrible midnight meetings. And Calormenes are never good woodsmen. Poggin thought that even by daylight they could easily get round to somewhere behind the stable without being seen. This would be much harder to do when the night had come and the Ape might be calling the Beasts together and all the Calormenes were on duty. And when the meeting did begin they could leave Puzzle at the back of the stable, completely out of sight, till the moment at which they wanted to produce him. This was obviously a good thing: for their only chance was to give the Narnians a sudden surprise.

Everyone agreed and the whole party set off on a new line – North-West – towards the hated Hill. The Eagle sometimes flew to and fro above them, sometimes he sat perched on Puzzle's back. No one – not even the King himself except in some great need – would dream of *riding* on a Unicorn.

This time Jill and Eustace walked together. They had been feeling very brave when they were begging to be allowed to come with the others, but now they didn't feel brave at all.

"Pole," said Eustace in a whisper. "I may as well tell you I've got the wind up."

"Oh *you're* all right, Scrubb," said Jill. "You can fight. But I – I'm just shaking, if you want to know the truth."

"Oh shaking's nothing," said Eustace. "I'm feeling I'm going to be sick."

"Don't talk about *that*, for goodness' sake," said Jill.

They went on in silence for a minute or two.

"Pole," said Eustace presently.

"What?" said she.

"What'll happen if we get killed here?"

"Well we'll be dead, I suppose."

"But I mean, what will happen in our own world? Shall we wake up and find ourselves back in that train? Or shall we just vanish and never be heard of any more? Or shall we be dead in England?"

"Gosh. I never thought of that."

"It'll be rum for Peter and the others if they saw me waving out of the window and then when the train comes in we're nowhere to be found! Or if they found two – I mean, if we're dead over there in England."

"Ugh!" said Jill. "What a horrid idea."

"It wouldn't be horrid for *us*," said Eustace. "We shouldn't be there."

"I almost wish – no I don't, though," said Jill.

"What were you going to say?"

"I *was* going to say I wished we'd never come. But I don't, I don't, I don't. Even if we *are* killed. I'd rather be killed fighting for Narnia than grow old and stupid at home and perhaps go about in a bath-chair and then die in the end just the same."

"Or be smashed up by British Railways!"

"Why d'you say that?"

"Well when that awful jerk came – the one that seemed to throw us into Narnia – I thought it *was* the beginning of a railway accident. So I was jolly glad to find ourselves here instead."

While Jill and Eustace were talking about this, the others were discussing their plans and becoming less miserable. That was because they were now thinking of what was to be done this very night and the thought of what had happened to Narnia – the thought that all her glories and joys were over – was pushed away into the back part of their minds. The moment they stopped talking it would come out and make them wretched again: but they kept on talking. Poggin was really quite cheerful about the night's work they had to do. He was sure that the Boar and the Bear, and probably all the Dogs would come over to their side at once. And he couldn't believe that all the other Dwarfs would stick to Griffle. And fighting by firelight and in and out among trees would be an advantage to the weaker side. And then, if they could win tonight, need they really throw their lives away by meeting the main Calormene army a few days later?

Why not hide in the woods, or even up in the Western Waste beyond the great waterfall and live like outlaws? And then they might gradually get stronger and stronger, for Talking Beasts and Archenlanders would be joining them every day. And at last they'd come out of hiding and sweep the Calormenes (who would have got careless by then) out of the country and Narnia would be revived. After all, something very like that had happened in the time of King Miraz!

And Tirian heard all this and thought "But what about Tash?" and felt in his bones that none of it was going to happen. But he didn't say so.

When they got nearer to Stable Hill of course everyone became quiet. Then the real wood-work began. From the moment at which they first saw the Hill to the moment at which they all arrived at the back of the stable, it took them over two hours. It's the sort of thing one couldn't describe properly unless one wrote pages and pages about it. The journey from each bit of cover to the next was a separate adventure, and there were very long waits in between, and several false alarms. If you are a good Scout or a good Guide you will know already what it must have been like. By about sunset they were all safe in a clump of holly trees about fifteen yards

behind the stable. They all munched some biscuit and lay down.

Then came the worst part, the waiting. Luckily for the children they slept for a couple of hours, but of course they woke up when the night grew cold, and what was worse, woke up very thirsty and with no chance of getting a drink. Puzzle just stood, shivering a little with nervousness, and said nothing. But Tirian, with his head against Jewel's flank, slept as soundly as if he were in his royal bed at Cair Paravel, till the sound of a gong beating awoke him and he sat up and saw that there was firelight on the far side of the stable and knew that the hour had come.

"Kiss me, Jewel," he said. "For certainly this is our last night on earth. And if ever I offended against you in any matter great or small, forgive me now."

"Dear King," said the Unicorn, "I could almost wish you had, so that I might forgive it. Farewell. We have known great joys together. If Aslan gave me my choice I would choose no other life than the life I have had and no other death than the one we go to."

Then they woke up Farsight, who was asleep with his head under his wing (it made him look as if he had no head at all), and crept forward to the stable. They left Puzzle (not without a kind word, for no one was angry with him now) just behind it, telling him not to move till someone came to fetch him, and took up their position at one end of the stable.

The bonfire had not been lit for long and was just beginning to blaze up. It was only a few feet away from them, and the great crowd of Narnian creatures were on the other side of it, so that Tirian could not at first see them very well, though of course he saw dozens of eyes shining with the reflection of the fire, as you've seen a rabbit's or cat's eyes in the headlights of a car. And just as Tirian took his place, the gong stopped beating and from somewhere on his left three figures appeared. One was Rishda Tarkaan the Calormene Captain. The second was the Ape. He was holding on to the Tarkaan's hand with one paw and kept whimpering and muttering, "Not so fast, don't go so fast, I'm not *at all* well. Oh my poor head! These midnight meetings are getting too much for me. Apes aren't meant to be up at night: It's not as if I was a rat or a bat – oh my poor head." On the other side of the Ape, walking very soft and stately, with his tail straight up in the air, came Ginger the Cat. They were heading for the bonfire and were so close to Tirian that they would have seen him at once if they had looked in the right direction. Fortunately they did not. But Tirian heard Rishda say to Ginger in a low voice:

"Now, Cat, to thy post. See thou play thy part well."

"Miaow, miaow. Count on me!" said Ginger. Then he stepped away beyond the bonfire and sat down in the front

row of the assembled Beasts: in the audience, as you might say.

For really, as it happened, the whole thing was rather like a theatre. The crowd of Narnians were like the people in the seats; the little grassy place just in front of the stable, where the bonfire burned and the Ape and the Captain stood to talk to the crowd, was like the stage; the stable itself was like the scenery at the back of the stage; and Tirian and his friends were like people peering round from behind the scenery. It was a splendid position. If any of them stepped forward into the full firelight, all eyes would be fixed on him at once: on the other hand, so long as they stood still in the shadow of the end-wall of the stable, it was a hundred to one against their being noticed.

Rishda Tarkaan dragged the Ape up close to the fire. The pair of them turned to face the crowd, and this of course meant that their backs were towards Tirian and his friends.

"Now, Monkey," said Rishda Tarkaan in a low voice. "Say the words that wiser heads have put into thy mouth. And hold up thy head." As he spoke he gave the Ape a little prod or kick from behind with the point of his toe.

"Do leave me alone," muttered Shift. But he sat up straighter and began, in a louder voice — "Now listen, all of you. A terrible thing has happened. A wicked thing. The wickedest thing that ever was done in Narnia. And Aslan —"

"Tashlan, fool," whispered Rishda Tarkaan.

"Tashlan I mean, of course," said the Ape, "is very angry about it."

There was a terrible silence while the Beasts waited to hear what new trouble was in store for them. The little party by the end-wall of the stable also held their breath. What on earth was coming now?

"Yes," said the Ape. "At this very moment, when the Terrible One himself is among us – there in the stable just behind me – one wicked Beast has chosen to do what you'd think no one would dare to do even if *He* were a thousand miles away. It has dressed itself up in a lion-skin and is wandering about in these very woods pretending to be Aslan."

Jill wondered for a moment if the Ape had gone mad. Was he going to tell the whole truth? A roar of horror and rage went up from the Beasts. "Grrr!" came the growls. "Who is he? Where is he? Just let me get my teeth into him!"

"It was seen last night," screamed the Ape, "but it got away. It's a Donkey! A common, miserable Ass! If any of you see that Ass –"

"Grrr!" growled the Beasts. "We will, we will. He'd better keep out of *our* way."

Jill looked at the King: his mouth was open and his face was full of horror. And then she understood the devilish cunning of the enemies' plan. By mixing a little truth with it they had made their lie far stronger. What was the good, now, of telling the Beasts that an ass had been dressed up as a lion to deceive them? The Ape would only say, "That's just what I've said." What was the good of showing them Puzzle in his lion-skin? They would only tear him in pieces. "That's taken the wind out of our sails," whispered Eustace. "The ground is taken from under our feet," said Tirian. "Cursed, cursed cleverness!" said Poggin. "I'll be sworn that this new lie is of Ginger's making."

CHAPTER TEN

WHO WILL GO INTO THE STABLE?

JILL felt something tickling her ear. It was Jewel the Unicorn, whispering to her with the wide whisper of a horse's mouth. As soon as she heard what he was saying she nodded and tip-toed back to where Puzzle was standing. Quickly and quietly she cut the last cords that bound the lion-skin to him. It wouldn't do for him to be caught with *that* on, after what the Ape had said! She would like to have hidden the skin somewhere very far away, but it was too heavy. The best she could do was to kick it in among the thickest bushes. Then she made signs to Puzzle to follow her and they both joined the others.

The Ape was speaking again.

"And after a horrid thing like that, Aslan – Tashlan – is angrier than ever. He says he's been a great deal too good to you, coming out every night to be looked at, see! Well, he's not coming out any more."

Howls and mewings and squeals and grunts were the Animals' answer to this, but suddenly a quite different voice broke in with a loud laugh.

"Hark what the monkey says," it shouted. "We know why he isn't going to bring his precious Aslan out. I'll tell you why: because he hasn't got him. He never had anything except an old donkey with a lion-skin on its back. Now he's lost *that* and he doesn't know what to do."

Tirian could not see the faces on the other side of the fire very well but he guessed this was Griffle the Chief Dwarf. And he was quite certain of it when, a second later, all the Dwarfs' voices joined in, singing: "Don't know what to do! Don't know what to do! Don't know what to do-o-o!"

"Silence!" thundered Rishda Tarkaan. "Silence, children of mud! Listen to me, you other Narnians, lest I give command to my warriors to fall upon you with the edge of the sword. The Lord Shift has already told you of that wicked Ass. Do you think, because of him that there is no *real* Tashlan in the stable! Do you? Beware, beware."

"No, no," shouted most of the crowd. But the Dwarfs said, "That's right, Darkie, you've got it. Come on, Monkey, show us what's in the stable, seeing is believing."

When next there was a moment's quiet the Ape said:

"You Dwarfs think you're very clever, don't you? But not so fast. I never said you couldn't see Tashlan. Anyone who likes can see him."

The whole assembly became silent. Then, after nearly a minute, the Bear began in a slow, puzzled voice:

"I don't quite understand all this," it grumbled, "I thought you said –"

"*You* thought!" repeated the Ape. "As if anyone could call what goes on in your head *thinking*. Listen, you others. Anyone can see Tashlan. But he's not coming out. You have to go in and see *him*."

"Oh, thank you, thank you, thank you," said dozens of voices. "That's what we wanted! We can go in and see him face to face. And now he'll be kind and it will all be as it used to be." And the Birds chattered, and the Dogs barked excitedly. Then suddenly, there was a great stirring and a noise of creatures rising to their feet, and in a second the whole lot of them would have been rushing forward and trying to crowd into the stable door all together. But the Ape shouted:

"Get back! Quiet! Not so fast."

The Beasts stopped, many of them with one paw in the air, many with tails wagging, and all of them with heads on one side.

"I thought you said," began the Bear, but Shift interrupted.

"Anyone can go in," he said. "But, one at a time. Who'll go first? He didn't *say* he was feeling very kind. He's been licking his lips a lot since he swallowed up the wicked King the other night. He's been growling a good deal this morning. I wouldn't much like to go into that stable myself tonight. But just as you please. Who'd like to go in first? Don't blame me if he swallows you whole or blasts you into a cinder with the mere terror of his eyes. That's your affair. Now then! Who's first? What about one of you Dwarfs?"

"Dilly, dilly, come and be killed!" sneered Griffle. "How do we know what you've got in there?"

"Ho-ho!" cried the Ape. "So you're beginning to think there's *something* there, eh? Well, all you Beasts were making noise enough a minute ago. What's struck you all dumb? Who's going in first?"

But the Beasts all stood looking at one another and began backing away from the stable. Very few tails were wagging now. The Ape waddled to and fro jeering at them. "Ho-ho-ho!" he chuckled. "I thought you were all so eager to see Tashlan face to face! Changed your mind, eh?"

Tirian bent his head to hear something that Jill was trying to whisper in his ear. "What do you think is really inside the stable?" she said. "Who knows?" said Tirian. "Two Calormenes with drawn swords, as likely as not, one

on each side of the door." "You don't think," said Jill, "it might be ... you know ... that horrid thing we saw?" "Tash himself?" whispered Tirian. "There's no knowing. But courage, child: we are all between the paws of the true Aslan."

Then a most surprising thing happened. Ginger the Cat said in a cool, clear voice, not at all as if he was excited, "I'll go in, if you like."

Every creature turned and fixed its eyes on the Cat. "Mark their subtleties, Sire," said Poggin to the King. "This cursed cat is in the plot, in the very centre of it. Whatever is in the stable will not hurt him, I'll be bound. Then Ginger will come out again and say that he has seen some wonder."

But Tirian had no time to answer him. The Ape was calling the Cat to come forward. "Ho-ho!" said the Ape. "So you, a pert Puss, would look upon him face to face. Come on, then! I'll open the door for you. Don't blame me if he scares the whiskers off your face. That's your affair."

And the Cat got up and came out of its place in the crowd, walking primly and daintily, with its tail in the air, not one hair on its sleek coat out of place. It came on till it had passed the fire and was so close that Tirian, from where he stood with his shoulder against the end-wall of the stable, could look right into its face. Its big green eyes never blinked. ("Cool as a cucumber," muttered Eustace. "*It* knows it has nothing to fear.") The Ape, chuckling and making faces, shuffled across beside the Cat: put up his paw: drew the bolt and opened the door. Tirian thought he could hear the Cat purring as it walked into the dark doorway.

"Aii-aii-aouwee! –" The most horrible caterwaul you ever heard made everyone jump. You have been wakened yourself by cats quarrelling or making love on the roof in the middle of the night: you know the sound.

This was worse. The Ape was knocked head over heels by Ginger coming back out of the stable at top speed. If you had not known he was a cat, you might have thought he was a ginger-coloured streak of lightning. He shot across the open grass, back into the crowd. No one wants to meet a cat in that state. You could see animals getting out of his way to left and right. He dashed up a tree, whisked around, and hung head downwards. His tail was bristled out till it was nearly as thick as his whole body: his eyes were like saucers of green fire: along his back every single hair stood on end.

"I'd give my beard," whispered Poggin, "to know whether that brute is only acting or whether it has really found something in there that frightened it!"

"Peace, friend," said Tirian, for the Captain and the Ape were also whispering and he wanted to hear what they said. He did not succeed, except that he heard the Ape once more whimpering "My head, my head," but he got the idea that those two were almost as puzzled by the cat's behaviour as himself.

"Now, Ginger," said the Captain. "Enough of that noise. Tell them what thou hast seen."

"Aii – Aii – Aaow – Awah," screamed the Cat.

"Art thou not called a *Talking* Beast?" said the Captain. "Then hold thy devilish noise and talk."

What followed was rather horrible. Tirian felt quite certain (and so did the others) that the Cat was trying to

say something: but nothing came out of his mouth except the ordinary, ugly cat-noises you might hear from any angry or frightened old Tom in a backyard in England. And the longer he caterwauled the less like a Talking Beast he looked. Uneasy whimperings and little sharp squeals broke out from among the other Animals.

"Look, look!" said the voice of the Bear. "It can't talk. It has forgotten how to talk! It has gone back to being a dumb beast. Look at its face." Everyone saw that it was true. And then the greatest terror of all fell upon those Narnians. For every one of them had been taught – when it was only a chick or a puppy or a cub – how Aslan at the beginning of the world had turned the beasts of Narnia into Talking Beasts and warned them that if they weren't good they might one day be turned back again and be like the poor witless animals one meets in other countries. "And now it is coming upon us," they moaned.

"Mercy! Mercy!" wailed the Beasts. "Spare us, Lord Shift, stand between us and Aslan, you must always go in and speak to him for us. We daren't, we daren't."

Ginger disappeared further up into the tree. No one ever saw him again.

Tirian stood with his hand on his sword-hilt and his head bowed. He was dazed with the horrors of that night. Sometimes he thought it would be best to draw his sword at once and rush upon the Calormenes: then next moment he thought it would be better to wait and see what new turn affairs might take. And now a new turn came.

"My Father," came a clear, ringing voice from the left of the crowd. Tirian knew at once that it was one of the Calormenes speaking, for in The Tisroc's army the common soldiers call the officers "My Master" but the officers call their senior officers "My Father". Jill and Eustace didn't know this but, after looking this way and that, they saw the speaker, for of course people at the sides of the crowd were easier to see than people in the middle where the glare of the fire made all beyond it look rather black. He was young and tall and slender, and even rather beautiful in the dark, haughty, Calormene way.

"My Father," he said to the Captain, "I also desire to go in."

"Peace, Emeth," said the Captain, "Who called thee to counsel? Does it become a boy to speak?"

"My Father," said Emeth. "Truly I am younger than thou, yet I also am of the blood of the Tarkaans even as thou art, and I also am the servant of Tash. Therefore . . ."

"Silence," said Rishda Tarkaan. "Am not I thy Captain? Thou hast nothing to do with this stable. It is for the Narnians."

"Nay, my Father," answered Emeth. "Thou hast said that their Aslan and our Tash are all one. And if that is the truth, then Tash himself is in yonder. And how then sayest thou that I have nothing to do with him? For gladly would I die a thousand deaths if I might look once on the face of Tash."

"Thou art a fool and understandest nothing," said Rishda Tarkaan. "These be high matters."

Emeth's face grew sterner. "Is it then not true that Tash and Aslan are all one?" he asked. "Has the Ape lied to us?"

"Of course they're all one," said the Ape.

"Swear it, Ape," said Emeth.

"Oh dear!" whimpered Shift, "I wish you'd all stop bothering me. My head does ache. Yes, yes, I swear it."

"Then, my Father," said Emeth, "I am utterly determined to go in."

"Fool," began Rishda Tarkaan, but at once the Dwarfs began shouting: "Come along, Darkie. Why don't you let him in? Why do you let Narnians in and keep your own people out? What have you got in there that you don't want your own men to meet?"

Tirian and his friends could only see the back of Rishda Tarkaan, so they never knew what his face looked like as he shrugged his shoulders and said, "Bear witness all that I am guiltless of this young fool's blood. Get thee in, rash boy, and make haste."

Then, just as Ginger had done, Emeth came walking forward into the open strip of grass between the bonfire and the stable. His eyes were shining, his face very solemn, his hand was on his sword-hilt, and he carried his head high.

Jill felt like crying when she looked at his face. And Jewel whispered in the King's ear, "By the Lion's Mane, I almost love this young warrior, Calormene though he be. He is worthy of a better god than Tash."

"I do wish we knew what is really inside there," said Eustace.

Emeth opened the door and went in, into the black mouth of the stable. He closed the door behind him. Only a few moments passed — but it seemed longer — before the door opened again. A figure in Calormene armour reeled out, fell on its back, and lay still: the door closed behind it. The Captain leaped towards it and bent down to stare at its face. He gave a start of surprise. Then he recovered himself and turned to the crowd, crying out:

"The rash boy has had his will. He has looked on Tash and is dead. Take warning, all of you."

"We will, we will," said the poor Beasts. But Tirian and his friends stared at the dead Calormene and then at one another. For they, being so close, could see what the crowd, being further off and beyond the fire, could not see: this dead man was not Emeth. He was quite different: an older man, thicker and not so tall, with a big beard.

"Ho-ho-ho," chuckled the Ape. "Any more? Anyone

else want to go in? Well, as you're all shy, I'll choose the next. You, you Boar! On you come. Drive him up, Calormenes. He *shall* see Tashlan face to face."

"O-o-mph," grunted the Boar, rising heavily to his feet. "Come on, then. Try my tusks."

When Tirian saw that brave Beast getting ready to fight for its life — and Calormene soldiers beginning to close in on it with their drawn scimitars — and no one going to its help — something seemed to burst inside him. He no longer cared if this was the best moment to interfere or not.

"Swords out," he whispered to the others. "Arrow on string. Follow."

Next moment the astonished Narnians saw seven figures leap forth in front of the stable, four of them in shining mail. The King's sword flashed in the firelight as he waved it above his head and cried in a great voice:

"Here stand I, Tirian of Narnia, in Aslan's name, to prove with my body that Tash is a foul fiend, the Ape a manifold traitor, and these Calormenes worthy of death. To my side, all true Narnians. Would you wait till your new masters have killed you all one by one?"

CHAPTER ELEVEN

THE PACE QUICKENS

QUICK as lightning, Rishda Tarkaan leaped back out of reach of the King's sword. He was no coward, and would have fought single-handed against Tirian and the Dwarf if need were. But he could not take on the Eagle and the Unicorn as well. He knew how Eagles can fly into your face and peck at your eyes and blind you with their wings. And he had heard from his father (who had met Narnians in battle) that no man, except with arrows, or a long spear, can match a Unicorn, for it rears on its hind legs as it falls upon you and then you have its hoofs and its horn and its teeth to deal with all at once. So he rushed into the crowd and stood calling out:

"To me, to me, warriors of The Tisroc, may-he-live-forever. To me, all loyal Narnians, lest the wrath of Tashlan fall upon you!"

While this was happening two other things happened as well. The Ape had not realized his danger as quickly as the Tarkaan. For a second or so he remained squatting beside the fire staring at the newcomers. Then Tirian rushed upon the wretched creature, picked it up by the scruff of the neck, and dashed back to the stable shouting, "Open the door!" Poggin opened it. "Go and drink your own medicine, Shift!" said Tirian and hurled the Ape through into the darkness. But as the Dwarf banged the door shut again, a blinding greenish-blue light shone out from the inside of the stable, the earth shook, and there was a strange noise — a clucking and screaming as if it was the hoarse voice of some monstrous bird. The Beasts moaned and howled and called out "Tashlan! Hide us from him!" and many fell down, and many hid their faces in their wings or paws. No one except Farsight the Eagle, who has the best eyes of all living things, noticed the face of Rishda Tarkaan at that moment. And from what Farsight saw there he knew at once that Rishda was just as surprised, and nearly frightened, as everyone else. "There goes one," thought Farsight, "who has called on gods he does not believe in. How will it be with him if they have really come?"

The third thing – which also happened at the same moment – was the only really beautiful thing that night. Every single Talking Dog in the whole meeting (there were fifteen of them) came bounding and barking joyously to the King's side. They were mostly great big dogs with thick shoulders and heavy jaws. Their coming was like the breaking of a great wave on the sea-beach: it nearly knocked you down. For though they were Talking Dogs they were just as doggy as they could be: and they all stood up and put their front paws on the shoulders of the humans and licked their faces, all saying at once: "Welcome! Welcome! We'll help, we'll help, help, help. Show us how to help, show us how, how. How-how-how?"

It was so lovely that it made you want to cry. This,

at last, was the sort of thing they had been hoping for. And when, a moment later, several little animals (mice and moles and a squirrel or so) came pattering up, squealing with joy, and saying "See, see. We're here," and when, after that, the Bear and the Boar came too, Eustace began to feel that perhaps, after all, everything might be going to come right. But Tirian gazed round and saw how very few of the animals had moved.

"To me! to me!" he called. "Have you all turned cowards since I was your King?"

"We daren't," whimpered dozens of voices. "Tashlan would be angry. Shield us from Tashlan."

"Where are all the Talking Horses?" said Tirian to the Boar.

"We've seen, we've seen," squealed the Mice. "The Ape has made them work. They're all tied — down at the bottom of the hill."

"Then all you little ones," said Tirian, "you nibblers and gnawers and nutcrackers, away with you as fast as you can scamper and see if the Horses are on our side. And if they are, get your teeth into the ropes and gnaw till the Horses are free and bring them hither."

"With a good will, Sire," came the small voices, and with a whisk of tails those sharp-eyed and sharp-toothed folk were off. Tirian smiled for mere love as he saw them go. But it was already time to be thinking of other things. Rishda Tarkaan was giving his orders.

"Forward," he said. "Take all of them alive if you can and hurl them into the stable or drive them into it. When they are all in we will put fire to it and make them an offering to the great god Tash."

"Ha!" said Farsight to himself. "So that is how he hopes to win Tash's pardon for his unbelief."

The enemy line – about half of Rishda's force – was now moving forward, and Tirian had barely time to give his orders.

"Out on the left, Jill, and try to shoot all you may before they reach us. Boar and Bear next to her. Poggin on my left, Eustace on my right. Hold the right wing, Jewel. Stand by him, Puzzle, and use your hoofs. Hover and strike, Farsight. You Dogs, just behind us. Go in among them after the sword-play has begun. Aslan to our aid!"

Eustace stood with his heart beating terribly, hoping and hoping that he would be brave. He had never seen anything (though he had seen both a dragon and a sea-serpent) that made his blood run so cold as that line of dark-faced bright-eyed men. There were fifteen Calormenes, a Talking Bull of Narnia, Slinkey the Fox, and Wraggle the Satyr. Then he heard twang-and-zipp on his left and one Calormene fell: then twang-and-zipp again and the Satyr was down. "Oh, well done, daughter!" came Tirian's voice; and then the enemy were upon them.

Eustace could never remember what happened in the next two minutes. It was all like a dream (the sort you have when your temperature is over 100) until he heard Rishda Tarkaan's voice calling out from the distance:

"Retire. Back hither and re-form."

Then Eustace came to his senses and saw the Calormenes scampering back to their friends. But not all of them. Two lay dead, pierced by Jewel's horn, one by Tirian's sword. The Fox lay dead at his own feet, and he wondered if it was he who had killed it. The Bull also was down, shot through the eye by an arrow from Jill and gashed in his side by the Boar's tusk. But our side had its losses too. Three dogs were killed and a fourth was hobbling behind the line on three legs and whimpering. The Bear lay on the ground, moving feebly. Then it mumbled in its throaty voice, bewildered to the last, "I – I don't – understand," laid its big head down on the grass as quietly as a child going to sleep, and never moved again.

In fact, the first attack had failed. Eustace didn't seem able to be glad about it: he was so terribly thirsty and his arm ached so.

As the defeated Calormenes went back to their commander, the Dwarfs began jeering at them.

"Had enough, Darkies?" they yelled. "Don't you like it? Why doesn't your great Tarkaan go and fight himself instead of sending you to be killed? Poor Darkies!"

"Dwarfs," cried Tirian. "Come here and use your swords, not your tongues. There is still time. Dwarfs of Narnia! You can fight well, I know. Come back to your allegiance."

"Yah!" sneered the Dwarfs. "Not likely. You're just as

big humbugs as the other lot. We don't want any Kings.
The Dwarfs are for the Dwarfs. Boo!"

Then the Drum began: not a Dwarf drum this time, but
a big bull's hide Calormene drum. The children from the
very first hated the sound. *Boom – boom – ba-ba-boom* it
went. But they would have hated it far worse if they had
known what it meant. Tirian did. It meant that there were
other Calormene troops somewhere near and that Rishda
Tarkaan was calling them to his aid. Tirian and Jewel
looked at one another sadly. They had just begun to hope
that they might win that night: but it would be all over
with them if new enemies appeared.

Tirian gazed despairingly round. Several Narnians were
standing with the Calormenes, whether through treachery
or in honest fear of "Tashlan". Others were sitting still,
staring, not likely to join either side. But there were fewer
animals now: the crowd was much smaller. Clearly,
several of them had just crept quietly away during the
fighting.

Boom – boom – ba-ba-boom went the horrible drum.
Then another sound began to mix with it. "Listen!" said
Jewel: and then "Look!" said Farsight. A moment later
there was no doubt what it was. With a thunder of hoofs,
with tossing heads, widened nostrils, and waving manes,
over a score of Talking Horses of Narnia came charging
up the hill. The gnawers and nibblers had done their
work.

Poggin the Dwarf and the children opened their mouths
to cheer but that cheer never came. Suddenly the air was
full of the sound of twanging bow-strings and hissing
arrows. It was the Dwarfs who were shooting and – for a
moment Jill could hardly believe her eyes – they were
shooting the Horses. Dwarfs are deadly archers. Horse

after Horse rolled over. Not one of those noble Beasts ever reached the King.

"Little *Swine*," shrieked Eustace, dancing in his rage. "Dirty, filthy, treacherous little brutes." Even Jewel said, "Shall I run after those Dwarfs, Sire, and spit ten of them on my horn at each plunge?" But Tirian with his face as stern as stone, said, "Stand fast, Jewel. If you must weep, sweetheart (this was to Jill), turn your face aside and see you wet not your bow-string. And peace, Eustace. Do not scold, like a kitchen-girl. No warrior scolds. Courteous words or else hard knocks are his only language."

But the Dwarfs jeered back at Eustace. "That was a surprise for you, little boy, eh? Thought we were on *your* side, did you? No fear. We don't want any Talking Horses. We don't want you to win any more than the other gang. You can't take *us* in. The Dwarfs are for the Dwarfs."

Rishda Tarkaan was still talking to his men, doubtless making arrangements for the next attack and probably wishing he had sent his whole force into the first. The drum boomed on. Then, to their horror, Tirian and his friends heard, far fainter as if from a long way off, an answering drum. Another body of Calormenes had heard Rishda's signal and were coming to support him. You would not have known from Tirian's face that he had now given up all hope.

"Listen," he whispered in a matter-of-fact voice, "we must attack now, before yonder miscreants are strengthened by their friends."

"Bethink you, Sire," said Poggin, "that here we have the good wooden wall of the stable at our backs. If we advance, shall we not be encircled and get sword-points between our shoulders?"

"I would say as you do, Dwarf," said Tirian. "Were it not their very plan to force us into the stable? The further we are from its deadly door, the better."

"The King is right," said Farsight. "Away from this accursed stable, and whatever goblin lives inside it, at all costs."

"Yes, do let's," said Eustace. "I'm coming to hate the very sight of it."

"Good," said Tirian. "Now look yonder to our left. You see a great rock that gleams white like marble in the firelight. First we will fall upon those Calormenes. You, maiden, shall move out on our left and shoot as fast as ever you may into their ranks: and you, Eagle, fly at their faces from the right. Meanwhile we others will be charging them. When we are so close, Jill, that you can no longer shoot at them for fear of striking us, go back to the white rock and wait. You others, keep your ears wide even in the fighting. We must put them to flight in a few minutes or else not at all, for we are fewer than they. As soon as I call *Back*, then rush to join Jill at the white rock, where we shall have protection behind us and can breathe awhile. Now, be off, Jill."

Feeling terribly alone, Jill ran out about twenty feet, put her right leg back and her left leg forward, and set an arrow to her string. She wished her hands were not shaking so. "That's a rotten shot!" she said as her first arrow sped towards the enemy and flew over their heads. But she had another on the string next moment: she knew that speed was what mattered. She saw something big and black darting into the faces of the Calormenes. That was Farsight. First one man, and then another, dropped his sword and put up both his hands to defend his eyes. Then one of her own arrows hit a man, and another hit a Narnian wolf, who had, it seemed, joined the enemy. But she had been shooting only for a few seconds when she had to stop. With a flash of swords and of the Boar's tusks and Jewel's horn, and with deep baying from the dogs, Tirian and his party were rushing on their enemies, like men in a hundred yards' race. Jill was astonished to see how unprepared the Calormenes seemed to be. She did not realize that this was the result of her work and the Eagle's. Very few troops can keep on looking steadily to the front if they are getting arrows in their faces from one side and being pecked by an eagle on the other.

"Oh well done. *Well* done!" shouted Jill. The King's party were cutting their way right into the enemy. The Unicorn was tossing men as you'd toss hay on a fork. Even Eustace seemed to Jill (who after all didn't know very much about swordsmanship) to be fighting brilliantly. The Dogs were at the Calormenes' throats. It was going to work! It was victory at last – With a horrible, cold shock Jill noticed a strange thing. Though Calormenes were falling at each Narnian sword-stroke, they never seemed to get any fewer. In fact, there were actually more of them now than when the fight began. There were more every second. They were running up from every side. They were new Calormenes. These new ones had spears. There was such a crowd of them that she could hardly see her own friends. Then she heard Tirian's voice crying:

"Back! To the rock!"

The enemy had been reinforced. The drum had done its work.

CHAPTER TWELVE

THROUGH THE STABLE DOOR

JILL ought to have been back at the white rock already but she had quite forgotten that part of her orders in the excitement of watching the fight. Now she remembered. She turned at once and ran to it, and arrived there barely a second before the others. It thus happened that all of them, for a moment, had their backs to the enemy. They all wheeled round the moment they had reached it. A terrible sight met their eyes.

A Calormene was running towards the stable door carrying something that kicked and struggled. As he came between them and the fire they could see clearly both the shape of the man and the shape of what he carried. It was Eustace.

Tirian and the Unicorn rushed out to rescue him. But the Calormene was now far nearer to the door then they. Before they had covered half the distance he had flung Eustace in and shut the door on him. Half a dozen more Calormenes had run up behind him. They formed a line on the open space before the stable. There was no getting at it now.

Even then Jill remembered to keep her face turned aside, well away from her bow. "Even if I can't stop blubbing, I *won't* get my string wet," she said.

"'Ware arrows," said Poggin suddenly.

Everyone ducked and pulled his helmet well over his nose. The Dogs crouched behind. But though a few arrows came their way it soon became clear that they were not being shot at. Griffle and his Dwarfs were at their archery again. This time they were coolly shooting at the Calormenes.

"Keep it up, boys!" came Griffle's voice. "All together. Carefully. We don't want Darkies any more than we want Monkeys – or Lions – or Kings. The Dwarfs are for the Dwarfs."

Whatever else you may say about Dwarfs, no one can say they aren't brave. They could easily have got away to some safe place. They preferred to stay and kill as many of both sides as they could, except when both sides were kind enough to save them trouble by killing one another. They wanted Narnia for their own.

What perhaps they had not taken into account was that the Calormenes were mail-clad and the Horses had had no protection. Also the Calormenes had a leader. Rishda Tarkaan's voice cried out:

"Thirty of you keep watch on those fools by the white rock. The rest, after me, that we may teach these sons of earth a lesson."

Tirian and his friends, still panting from their fight and thankful for a few minutes' rest, stood and looked on while the Tarkaan led his men against the Dwarfs. It was a strange scene by now. The fire had sunk lower: the light it gave was now less and of a darker red. As far as one could see, the whole place of assembly was now empty except for the Dwarf and the Calormenes. In that light one couldn't make out much of what was happening. It sounded as if the Dwarfs were putting up a good fight. Tirian could hear Griffle using dreadful language, and every now and then the Tarkaan calling, "Take all you can alive! Take them alive!"

Whatever that fight may have been like, it did not last long. The noise of it died away. Then Jill saw the Tarkaan coming back to the stable: eleven men followed him, dragging eleven bound Dwarfs. (Whether the others had all been killed, or whether some of them had got away, was never known.)

"Throw them into the shrine of Tash," said Rishda Tarkaan.

And when the eleven Dwarfs, one after the other, had been flung or kicked into that dark doorway and the door had been shut again, he bowed low to the stable and said:

"These also are for thy burnt offering, Lord Tash."

And all the Calormenes banged the flats of their swords on their shields and shouted, "Tash! Tash! The great god Tash! Inexorable Tash!" (There was no nonsense about "Tashlan" now.)

The little party by the white rock watched these doings and whispered to one another. They had found a trickle of water coming down the rock and all had drunk eagerly – Jill and Poggin and the King in their hands, while the four-footed ones lapped from the little pool which it had made at the foot of the stone. Such was their thirst that it seemed the most delicious drink they had ever had in their lives, and while they were drinking they were perfectly happy and could not think of anything else.

"I feel in my bones," said Poggin, "that we shall all, one by one, pass through that dark door before morning. I can think of a hundred deaths I would rather have died."

"It is indeed a grim door," said Tirian. "It is more like a mouth."

"Oh, can't we do *anything* to stop it?" said Jill in a shaken voice.

"Nay, fair friend," said Jewel, nosing her gently. "It

may be for us the door to Aslan's country and we shall sup at his table tonight."

Rishda Tarkaan turned his back on the stable and walked slowly to a place in front of the white rock.

"Hearken," he said. "If the Boar and the Dogs and the Unicorn will come over to me and put themselves in my mercy, their lives shall be spared. The Boar shall go to a cage in The Tisroc's garden, the Dogs to The Tisroc's kennels, and the Unicorn, when I have sawn his horn off, shall draw a cart. But the Eagle, the children, and he who was the King shall be offered to Tash this night."

The only answer was growls.

"Get on, warriors," said the Tarkaan. "Kill the beasts, but take the two-legged ones alive."

And then the last battle of the last King of Narnia began.

What made it hopeless, even apart from the numbers of the enemy, was the spears. The Calormenes who had been with the Ape almost from the beginning had had no spears: that was because they had come into Narnia by ones and twos, pretending to be peaceful merchants, and of course they had carried no spears for a spear is not a thing you can hide. The new ones must have come in later, after the Ape was already strong and they could march openly. The spears made all the difference. With a long spear you can kill a boar before you are in reach of his tusks and a unicorn before you are in reach of his horn; if you are very quick and keep your head. And now the levelled spears were closing in on Tirian and his last friends. Next minute they were all fighting for their lives.

In a way it wasn't quite so bad as you might think.

When you are using every muscle to the full — ducking under a spear-point here, leaping over it there, lunging forward, drawing back, wheeling round — you haven't much time to feel either frightened or sad. Tirian knew he could do nothing for the others now; they were all doomed together. He vaguely saw the Boar go down on one side of him, and Jewel fighting furiously on the other. Out of the corner of one eye he saw, but only just saw, a big Calormene pulling Jill away somewhere by her hair. But he hardly thought about any of these things. His only thought now was to sell his life as dearly as he could. The worst of it was that he couldn't keep to the position in which he had started, under the white rock. A man who is fighting a dozen enemies at once must take his chances wherever he can; must dart in wherever he sees an enemy's breast or neck unguarded. In a very few strokes this may get you quite a distance from the spot where you began. Tirian soon found that he was getting further and further to the right, nearer to the stable. He had a vague idea in his mind that there was some good reason for keeping away from it. But he couldn't now remember what the reason was. And anyway, he couldn't help it.

All at once everything came quite clear. He found he was fighting the Tarkaan himself. The bonfire (what was left of it) was straight in front. He was in fact fighting in the very doorway of the stable, for it had been opened and two Calormenes were holding the door, ready to slam it shut the moment he was inside. He remembered everything now, and he realized that the enemy had been edging him to the stable on purpose ever since the fight began. And while he was thinking this he was still fighting the Tarkaan as hard as he could.

A new idea came into Tirian's head. He dropped his sword, darted forward, in under the sweep of the Tarkaan's scimitar, seized his enemy by the belt with both hands, and jumped back into the stable, shouting:

"Come in and meet Tash yourself!"

There was a deafening noise. As when the Ape had been flung in, the earth shook and there was a blinding light.

The Calormene soldiers outside screamed. "Tash, Tash!" and banged the door. If Tash wanted their own Captain, Tash must have him. They, at any rate, did not want to meet Tash.

For a moment or two Tirian did not know where he was or even who he was. Then he steadied himself, blinked, and looked around. It was not dark inside the stable, as he had expected. He was in strong light: that was why he was blinking.

He turned to look at Rishda Tarkaan, but Rishda was not looking at him. Rishda gave a great wail and pointed; then he put his hands before his face and fell flat, face downwards, on the ground. Tirian looked in the direction where the Tarkaan had pointed. And then he understood.

A terrible figure was coming towards them. It was far smaller than the shape they had seen from the Tower, though still much bigger than a man, and it was the same. It had a vulture's head and four arms. Its beak was open and its eyes blazed. A croaking voice came from its beak.

"Thou hast called me into Narnia, Rishda Tarkaan. Here I am. What hast thou to say?"

But the Tarkaan neither lifted his face from the ground nor said a word. He was shaking like a man with a bad

hiccup. He was brave enough in battle: but half his courage had left him earlier that night when he first began to suspect that there might be a real Tash. The rest of it had left him now.

With a sudden jerk — like a hen stooping to pick up a worm — Tash pounced on the miserable Rishda and tucked him under the upper of his two right arms. Then Tash turned his head sidewise to fix Tirian with one of his terrible eyes: for of course, having a bird's head, he couldn't look at you straight.

But immediately, from behind Tash, strong and calm as the summer sea, a voice said:

"Begone, Monster, and take your lawful prey to your own place: in the name of Aslan and Aslan's great Father the Emperor-over-the-Sea."

The hideous creature vanished, with the Tarkaan still under its arm. And Tirian turned to see who had spoken.

And what he saw then set his heart beating as it had never beaten in any fight.

Seven Kings and Queens stood before him, all with crowns on their heads and all in glittering clothes, but the Kings wore fine mail as well and had their swords drawn in their hands. Tirian bowed courteously and was about to speak when the youngest of the Queens laughed. He stared hard at her face, and then gasped with amazement, for he knew her. It was Jill: but not Jill as he had last seen her, with her face all dirt and tears and an old drill dress half slipping off one shoulder. Now she looked cool and fresh, as fresh as if she had just come from bathing. And at first he thought she looked older, but then didn't, and he could never make up his mind on that point. And then he saw that the youngest of the Kings was Eustace: but he also was changed as Jill was changed.

Tirian suddenly felt awkward about coming among these people with the blood and dust and sweat of a battle still on him. Next moment he realized that he was not in that state at all. He was fresh and cool and clean, and dressed in such clothes as he would have worn for a great feast at Cair Paravel. (But in Narnia your good clothes were never your uncomfortable ones. They knew how to make things that felt beautiful as well as looking beautiful in Narnia: and there was no such thing as starch or flannel or elastic to be found from one end of the country to the other.)

"Sire," said Jill coming forward and making a beautiful curtsey, "let me make you known to Peter the High King over all Kings in Narnia."

Tirian had no need to ask which was the High King, for he remembered his face (though here it was far nobler) from his dream. He stepped forward, sank on one knee and kissed Peter's hand.

"High King," he said. "You are welcome to me."

And the High King raised him and kissed him on both cheeks as a High King should. Then he led him to the eldest of the Queens – but even she was not old, and there

were no grey hairs on her head and no wrinkles on her cheek – and said, "Sir, this is that Lady Polly who came into Narnia on the First Day, when Aslan made the trees grow and the Beasts talk." He brought him next to a man whose golden beard flowed over his breast and whose face was full of wisdom. "And this," he said, "is the Lord Digory who was with her on that day. And this is my brother, King Edmund: and this my sister, the Queen Lucy."

"Sir," said Tirian, when he had greeted all these. "If I have read the chronicle aright, there should be another. Has not your Majesty two sisters? Where is Queen Susan?"

"My sister Susan," answered Peter shortly and gravely,

"is no longer a friend of Narnia."

"Yes," said Eustace, "and whenever you've tried to get her to come and talk about Narnia or do anything about Narnia, she says, 'What wonderful memories you have! Fancy your still thinking about all those funny games we used to play when we were children.'"

"Oh Susan!" said Jill. "She's interested in nothing nowadays except nylons and lipstick and invitations. She always was a jolly sight too keen on being grown-up."

"Grown-up, indeed," said the Lady Polly. "I wish she *would* grow up. She wasted all her school time wanting to be the age she is now, and she'll waste all the rest of her life trying to stay that age. Her whole idea is to race on to the silliest time of one's life as quick as she can and then stop there as long as she can."

"Well, don't let's talk about that now," said Peter. "Look! Here are lovely fruit-trees. Let us taste them."

And then, for the first time, Tirian looked about him and realized how very queer this adventure was.

CHAPTER THIRTEEN

HOW THE DWARFS REFUSED
TO BE TAKEN IN

TIRIAN had thought – or he would have thought if he
had time to think at all – that they were inside a little
thatched stable, about twelve feet long and six feet wide.
In reality they stood on grass, the deep blue sky was overhead, and the air which blew gently on their faces was
that of a day in early summer. Not far away from them
rose a grove of trees, thickly leaved, but under every leaf
there peeped out the gold or faint yellow or purple or
glowing red of fruits such as no one has seen in our
world. The fruit made Tirian feel that it must be autumn
but there was something in the feel of the air that told
him it could not be later than June. They all moved
towards the trees.

Everyone raised his hand to pick the fruit he best liked
the look of, and then everyone paused for a second. This
fruit was so beautiful that each felt "It can't be meant for
me . . . surely we're not allowed to pluck it."

"It's all right," said Peter. "I know what we're all
thinking. But I'm sure, quite sure, we needn't. I've a
feeling we've got to the country where everything is
allowed."

"Here goes, then!" said Eustace. And they all began to
eat.

What was the fruit like? Unfortunately no one can
describe a taste. All I can say is that, compared with those
fruits, the freshest grapefruit you've ever eaten was dull,
and the juiciest orange was dry, and the most melting
pear was hard and woody, and the sweetest wild

strawberry was sour. And there were no seeds or stones, and no wasps. If you had once eaten that fruit, all the nicest things in this world would taste like medicines after it. But I can't describe it. You can't find out what it is like unless you can get to that country and taste it for yourself.

When they had eaten enough, Eustace said to King Peter, "You haven't yet told us how you got here. You were just going to, when King Tirian turned up."

"There's not much to tell," said Peter. "Edmund and I were standing on the platform and we saw your train coming in. I remember thinking it was taking the bend far too fast. And I remember thinking how funny it was that our people were probably in the same train though Lucy didn't know about it –"

"Your people, High King?" said Tirian.

"I mean my Father and Mother – Edmund's and Lucy's and mine."

"Why were they?" asked Jill. "You don't mean to say *they* know about Narnia?"

"Oh no, it had nothing to do with Narnia. They were on their way to Bristol. I'd only heard they were going that morning. But Edmund said they'd be bound to be going by that train." (Edmund was the sort of person who knows about railways.)

"And what happened then?" said Jill.

"Well, it's not very easy to describe, is it, Edmund?" said the High King.

"Not very," said Edmund. "It wasn't at all like that other time when we were pulled out of our own world by Magic. There was a frightful roar and something hit me with a bang, but it didn't hurt. And I felt not so much scared as – well, excited. Oh – and this is one queer thing.

I'd had a rather sore knee, from a hack at rugger. I noticed it had suddenly gone. And I felt very light. And then – here we were."

"It was much the same for us in the railway carriage," said the Lord Digory, wiping the last traces of the fruit from his golden beard. "Only I think you and I, Polly, chiefly felt that we'd been unstiffened. You youngsters won't understand. But we stopped feeling old."

"Youngsters, indeed!" said Jill. "I don't believe you two really are much older than we are here."

"Well if we aren't, we have been," said the Lady Polly.

"And what has been happening since you got here?" asked Eustace.

"Well," said Peter, "for a long time (at least I suppose it was a long time) nothing happened. Then the door opened –"

"The door?" said Tirian.

"Yes," said Peter. "The door you came in – or came out – by. Have you forgotten?"

"But where is it?"

"Look," said Peter and pointed.

Tirian looked and saw the queerest and most ridiculous thing you can imagine. Only a few yards away, clear to be seen in the sunlight, there stood up a rough wooden door and, round it, the framework of the doorway: nothing else, no walls, no roof. He walked towards it, bewildered, and the others followed, watching to see what he would do. He walked round to the other side of the door. But it looked just the same from the other side: he was still in the open air, on a summer morning. The door was simply standing up by itself as if it had grown there like a tree.

"Fair Sir," said Tirian to the High King, "this is a great marvel."

"It is the door you came through with that Calormene five minutes ago," said Peter smiling.

"But did I not come in out of the wood into the stable? Whereas this seems to be a door leading from nowhere to nowhere."

"It looks like that if you walk *round* it," said Peter. "But put your eye to that place where there is a crack between two of the planks and look *through*."

Tirian put his eye to the hole. At first he could see nothing but blackness. Then, at his eyes grew used to it, he saw the dull red glow of a bonfire that was nearly going out, and above that, in a black sky, stars. Then he could see dark figures moving about or standing between him and the fire: he could hear them talking and their voices were like those of Calormenes. So he knew that he was looking out through the stable door into the darkness of Lantern Waste where he had fought his last battle. The men were discussing whether to go in and look for Rishda Tarkaan (but none of them wanted to do that) or to set fire to the stable.

He looked round again and could hardly believe his eyes. There was the blue sky overhead, and grassy country spreading as far as he could see in every direction, and his new friends all round him laughing.

"It seems, then," said Tirian, smiling himself, "that the stable seen from within and the stable seen from without are two different places."

"Yes," said the Lord Digory. "Its inside is bigger than its outside."

"Yes," said Queen Lucy. "In our world too, a stable once had something inside it that was bigger than our whole world." It was the first time she had spoken, and from the thrill in her voice, Tirian now knew why. She was drinking everything in even more deeply than the others. She had been too happy to speak. He wanted to hear her speak again, so he said:

"Of your courtesy, Madam, tell on. Tell me your whole adventure."

"After the shock and the noise," said Lucy, "we found

ourselves here. And we wondered at the door, as you did. Then the door opened for the first time (we saw darkness through the doorway when it did) and there came through a big man with a naked sword. We saw by his arms that he was a Calormene. He took his stand beside the door with his sword raised, resting on his shoulder, ready to cut down anyone who came through. We went to him and spoke to him, but we thought he could neither see nor hear us. And he never looked round on the sky and the sunlight and the grass: I think he couldn't see them either. So then we waited a long time. Then we heard the bolt being drawn on the other side of the door. But the man didn't get ready to strike with his sword till he could see who was coming in. So we supposed he had been told to strike some and spare others. But at the very moment when the door opened, all of a sudden Tash was there, on this side of the door; none of us saw where he came from. And through the door there came a big Cat. It gave one look at Tash and ran for its life: just in time, for he pounced at it and the door hit his beak as it was shut. The man could see Tash. He turned very pale and bowed down before the Monster: but it vanished away.

"Then we waited a long time again. At last the door opened for the third time and there came in a young Calormene. I liked him. The sentinel at the door started, and looked very surprised, when he saw him. I think he'd been expecting someone quite different —"

"I see it all now," said Eustace (he had the bad habit of interrupting stories). "The Cat was to go in first and the sentry had orders to do him no harm. Then the Cat was to come out and say he'd seen their beastly Tashlan and *pretend* to be frightened so as to scare the other Animals. But what Shift never guessed was that the real Tash would turn up; so Ginger came out really frightened. And after that, Shift would send in anyone he wanted to get rid of and the sentry would kill them. And —"

"Friend," said Tirian softly, "you hinder the lady in her tale."

"Well," said Lucy, "the sentry was surprised. That gave the other man just time to get on guard. They had a fight. He killed the sentry and flung him outside the door. Then he came walking slowly forward to where we were. He could see us, and everything else. We tried to talk to him but he was rather like a man in a trance. He kept on saying Tash, Tash, where is Tash? I go to Tash. So we gave it up and he went away somewhere – over there. I liked him. And after that ... ugh!" Lucy made a face.

"After that," said Edmund, "someone flung a monkey through the door. And Tash was there again. My sister is so tender-hearted she doesn't like to tell you that Tash made one peck and the Monkey was gone!"

"Serve him right!" said Eustace. "All the same, I hope he'll disagree with Tash too."

"And after that," said Edmund, "came about a dozen Dwarfs: and then Jill, and Eustace, and last of all yourself."

"I hope Tash ate the Dwarfs too," said Eustace. "Little swine."

"No, he didn't," said Lucy. "And don't be horrid. Ther're still here. In fact you can see them from here. And I've tried and tried to make friends with them but it's no use."

"*Friends* with them!" cried Eustace. "If you knew how those Dwarfs have been behaving!"

"Oh stop it, Eustace," said Lucy. "Do come and see them. King Tirian, perhaps *you* could do something with them."

"I can feel no great love for Dwarfs today," said Tirian. "Yet at your asking, Lady, I would do a greater thing than this."

Lucy led the way and soon they could all see the Dwarfs. They had a very odd look. They weren't strolling about or enjoying themselves (although the cords with which they had been tied seemed to have vanished) nor were they lying down and having a rest. They were sitting very close together in a little circle facing one another. They never looked round or took any notice of the humans till Lucy and Tirian were almost near enough to touch them. Then the Dwarfs all cocked their heads as if they couldn't see anyone but were listening hard and trying to guess by the sound what was happening.

"Look out!" said one of them in a surly voice. "Mind where you're going. Don't walk into our faces!"

"All right!" said Eustace indignantly. "We're not blind. We've got eyes in our heads."

"They must be darn good ones if you can see in here," said the same Dwarf whose name was Diggle.

"In where?" asked Edmund.

"Why you bone-head, in *here* of course," said Diggle. "In this pitch-black, poky, smelly little hole of a stable."

"Are you blind?" said Tirian.

"Ain't we all blind in the dark!" said Diggle.

"But it isn't dark, you poor stupid Dwarfs," said Lucy. "Can't you see? Look up! Look round! Can't you see the sky and the trees and the flowers? Can't you see *me*?"

"How in the name of all Humbug can I see what ain't there? And how can I see you any more than you can see me in this pitch darkness?"

"But I *can* see you," said Lucy. "I'll prove I can see you. You've got a pipe in your mouth."

"Anyone that knows the smell of baccy could tell that," said Diggle.

"Oh the poor things! This is dreadful," said Lucy. Then she had an idea. She stopped and picked some wild violets. "Listen, Dwarf," she said. "Even if your eyes are wrong, perhaps your nose is all right: can you smell *that*?" She leaned across and held the fresh, damp flowers to Diggle's ugly nose. But she had to jump back quickly in order to avoid a blow from his hard little fist.

"None of that!" he shouted. "How dare you! What do you mean by shoving a lot of filthy stable-litter in my

face? There was a thistle in it too. It's like your sauce! And who are you anyway?"

"Earth-man," said Tirian, "she is the Queen Lucy, sent hither by Aslan out of the deep past. And it is for her sake alone that I, Tirian your lawful King, do not cut all your heads from your shoulders, proved and twice-proved traitors that you are."

"Well if that doesn't beat everything!" exclaimed Diggle. "How *can* you go on talking all that rot? Your wonderful Lion didn't come and help you, did he? Thought not. And now – even now – when you've been beaten and shoved into this black hole, just the same as the rest of us, you're still at your old game. Starting a new lie! Trying to make us believe we're none of us shut up, and it ain't dark, and heaven knows what."

"There *is* no black hole, save in your own fancy, fool," cried Tirian. "Come *out* of it." And, leaning forward, he caught Diggle by the belt and the hood and swung him right out of the circle of Dwarfs. But the moment Tirian put him down, Diggle darted back to his place among the others, rubbing his nose and howling:

"Ow! Ow! What d'you do that for! Banging my face against the wall. You've nearly broken my nose."

"Oh dear!" said Lucy, "What *are* we to do for them?"

"Let 'em alone," said Eustace: but as he spoke the earth trembled. The sweet air grew suddenly sweeter. A brightness flashed behind them. All turned. Tirian turned last because he was afraid. There stood his heart's desire, huge and real, the golden Lion, Aslan himself, and already the others were kneeling in a circle round his forepaws and burying their hands and faces in his mane as he stooped his great head to touch them with his tongue. Then he fixed his eyes upon Tirian, and Tirian came near, trembling, and flung himself at the Lion's feet, and the Lion kissed him and said, "Well done, last of the Kings of Narnia who stood firm at the darkest hour."

"Aslan," said Lucy through her tears, "could you — will you — do something for these poor Dwarfs?"

"Dearest," said Aslan, "I will show you both what I can, and what I cannot, do." He came close to the Dwarfs and gave a low growl: low, but it set all the air shaking. But the Dwarfs said to one another, "Hear that? That's the gang at the other end of the stable. Trying to frighten us. They do it with a machine of some kind. Don't take any notice. They won't take *us* in again!"

Aslan raised his head and shook his mane. Instantly a glorious feast appeared on the Dwarfs' knees: pies and tongues and pigeons and trifles and ices, and each Dwarf had a goblet of good wine in his right hand. But it wasn't much use. They began eating and drinking greedily enough, but it was clear that they couldn't taste it properly. They thought they were eating and drinking only the sort of things you might find in a stable. One said he was trying to eat hay and another said he had a bit of an old turnip and a third said he'd found a raw cabbage leaf. And they raised golden goblets of rich red wine to their lips and said "Ugh! Fancy drinking dirty water out of a trough that a donkey's been at! Never thought we'd come to this." But very soon every Dwarf began suspecting that every other Dwarf had found something nicer than he had, and they started grabbing and snatching, and went on to quarrelling, till in a few minutes there was a free fight and all the good food was smeared on their faces and clothes or trodden under foot. But when at last they sat down to nurse their black eyes and their bleeding noses, they all said:

"Well, at any rate there's no Humbug here. We haven't let anyone take us in. The Dwarfs are for the Dwarfs."

"You see, " said Aslan. "They will not let us help them. They have chosen cunning instead of belief. Their prison is only in their own minds, yet they are in that prison; and so afraid of being taken in that they cannot be taken out. But come, children. I have other work to do."

He went to the Door and they all followed him. He raised his head and roared, "Now it is time!" then louder, "Time!"; then so loud that it could have shaken the stars, "TIME." The Door flew open.

CHAPTER FOURTEEN

NIGHT FALLS ON NARNIA

THEY all stood beside Aslan, on his right side, and looked through the open doorway.

The bonfire had gone out. On the earth all was blackness: in fact you could not have told that you were looking into a wood if you had not seen where the dark shapes of the trees ended and the stars began. But when Aslan had roared yet again, out on their left they saw another black shape. That is, they saw another patch where there were no stars: and the patch rose up higher and higher and became the shape of a man, the hugest of all giants. They all knew Narnia well enough to work out where he must be standing. He must be on the high moorlands that stretch away to the North beyond the River Shribble. Then Jill and Eustace remembered how once long ago, in the deep caves beneath those moors, they had seen a great giant asleep and been told that his name was Father Time, and that he would wake on the day the world ended.

"Yes," said Aslan, though they had not spoken. "While he lay dreaming his name was Time. Now that he is awake he will have a new one."

Then the great giant raised a horn to his mouth. They could see this by the change of the black shape he made against the stars. After that – quite a bit later, because sound travels so slowly – they heard the sound of the horn: high and terrible, yet of a strange, deadly beauty.

Immediately the sky became full of shooting stars. Even one shooting star is a fine thing to see; but these were dozens, and then scores, and then hundreds, till it was like silver rain: and it went on and on. And when it had gone on for some while, one or two of them began to think that there was another dark shape against the sky as well as the giant's. It was in a different place, right overhead, up in the very roof of the sky as you might call it. "Perhaps it is a cloud," thought Edmund. At any rate, there were no stars there: just blackness. But all around, the downpour of stars went on. And then the starless patch began to grow, spreading further and further out from the centre of the sky. And presently a quarter of the whole sky was black, and then a half, and at last the rain of shooting stars was going on only low down near the horizon.

With a thrill of wonder (and there was some terror in it too) they all suddenly realized what was happening. The spreading blackness was not a cloud at all: it was simply emptiness. The black part of the sky was the part in which there were no stars left. All the stars were falling: Aslan had called them home.

The last few seconds before the rain of stars had quite ended were very exciting. Stars began falling all round them. But stars in that world are not the great flaming globes they are in ours. They are people (Edmund and Lucy had once met one). So now they found showers of glittering people, all with long hair like burning silver and spears like white-hot metal, rushing down to them out of the black air, swifter than falling stones. They made a hissing noise as they landed and burnt the grass. And all these stars glided past them and stood somewhere behind, a little to the right.

This was a great advantage, because otherwise, now that there were no stars in the sky, everything would have been completely dark and you could have seen nothing. As it was, the crowd of stars behind them cast a fierce, white light over their shoulders. They could see mile upon mile of Narnian woods spread out before them, looking as if they were floodlit. Every bush and almost every blade of grass had its black shadow behind it. The edge of every leaf stood out so sharp that you'd think you could cut your finger on it.

On the grass before them lay their own shadows. But the great thing was Aslan's shadow. It streamed away to their left, enormous and very terrible. And all this was under a sky that would now be starless forever.

The light from behind them (and a little to their right) was so strong that it lit up even the slopes of the Northern Moors. Something was moving there. Enormous animals were crawling and sliding down into Narnia: great dragons and giant lizards and featherless birds with wings like bats' wings. They disappeared into the woods and for a few minutes there was silence. Then there came – at first from very far off – sounds of wailing and then, from every direction, a rustling and a pattering and a sound of wings. It came nearer and nearer. Soon one could distinguish the scamper of little feet from the padding of big paws, and the clack-clack of light little hoofs from the thunder of great ones. And then one could see thousands of pairs of eyes gleaming. And at last, out of the shadow of the trees, racing up the hill for dear life, by thousands and by millions, came all kinds of creatures – Talking Beasts, Dwarfs, Satyrs, Fauns, Giants, Calormenes, men from Archenland, Monopods, and strange unearthly things from the remote islands of the unknown Western lands. And all these ran up to the doorway where Aslan stood.

This part of the adventure was the only one which seemed rather like a dream at the time and rather hard to remember properly afterwards. Especially, one couldn't say how long it had taken. Sometimes it seemed to have lasted only a few minutes, but at others it felt as if it might have gone on for years. Obviously, unless either the Door had grown very much larger or the creatures had suddenly grown as small as gnats, a crowd like that couldn't ever have tried to get through it. But no one thought about that sort of thing at the time.

The creatures came rushing on, their eyes brighter and brighter as they drew nearer and nearer to the standing Stars. But as they came right up to Aslan one or other of two things happened to each of them. They all looked straight in his face, I don't think they had any choice about that. And when some looked, the expression of their faces changed terribly — it was fear and hatred: except that, on the faces of Talking Bears, the fear and hatred lasted only for a fraction of a second. You could see that they suddenly ceased to the *Talking* Beasts. They were just ordinary animals. And all the creatures who looked at Aslan in that way swerved to their right, his left, and disappeared into his huge black shadow, which (as you have heard) streamed away to the left of the doorway. The children never saw them again. I don't know what became of them. But the others looked in the face of Aslan and loved him, though some of them were very frightened at the same time. And all these came in at the Door, in on Aslan's right. There were some queer specimens among them. Eustace even recognized one of those very Dwarfs who had helped to shoot the Horses. But he had no time to wonder about that sort of thing (and anyway it was no business of his) for a great joy put

everything else out of his head. Among the happy
creatures who now came crowding round Tirian and his
friends were all those whom they had thought dead.
There was Roonwit the Centaur and Jewel the Unicorn
and the good Boar and the good Bear, and Farsight the
Eagle, and the dear Dogs and the Horses, and Poggin the
Dwarf.

"Further in and higher up!" cried Roonwit and
thundered away in a gallop to the West. And though they
did not understand him, the words somehow set them
tingling all over. The Boar grunted at them cheerfully.
The Bear was just going to mutter that he still didn't
understand, when he caught sight of the fruit-trees behind
them. He waddled to those trees as fast as he could and
there, no doubt, found something he understood very
well. But the Dogs remained, wagging their tails, and
Poggin remained, shaking hands with everyone and
grinning all over his honest face. And Jewel leaned his
snowy white head over the King's shoulder and the King
whispered in Jewel's ear. Then everyone turned his
attention again to what could be seen through the
Doorway.

The Dragons and Giant Lizards now had Narnia to
themselves. They went to and fro tearing up the trees by
the roots and crunching them up as if they were sticks of
rhubarb. Minute by minute the forests disappeared. The
whole country became bare and you could see all sorts of
things about its shape – all the little humps and hollows –
which you had never noticed before. The grass died. Soon
Tirian found that he was looking at a world of bare rock
and earth. You could hardly believe that anything had
ever lived there. The monsters themselves grew old and
lay down and died. Their flesh shrivelled up and the

bones appeared: soon they were only huge skeletons that lay here and there on the dead rock, looking as if they had died thousands of years ago. For a long time everything was still.

At last something white – a long, level line of whiteness that gleamed in the light of the standing stars – came moving towards them from the Eastern end of the world.

A widespread noise broke the silence: first a murmur then a rumble, then a roar. And now they could see what it was that was coming, and how fast it came. It was a foaming wall of water. The sea was rising. In that tree-less world you could see it very well. You could see all the rivers getting wider and the lakes getting larger, and separate lakes joining into one, and valleys turning into new lakes, and hills turning into islands, and then those islands vanishing. And the high moors to their left and the higher mountains to their right crumbled and slipped down with a roar and a splash into the mounting water; and the water came swirling up to the very threshold of the Doorway (but never passed it) so that the foam splashed about Aslan's forefeet. All now was level water from where they stood to where the waters met the sky.

And out there it began to grow light. A streak of dreary and disastrous dawn spread along the horizon, and widened and grew brighter, till in the end they hardly noticed the light of the stars who stood behind them. At last the sun came up. When it did, the Lord Digory and the Lady Polly looked at one another and gave a little nod: those two, in a different world, had once seen a dying sun, and so they knew at once that this sun also was dying. It was three times – twenty times – as big as it ought to be, and very dark red. As its rays fell upon the great Time-giant, he turned red too: and in the reflection of that sun the whole waste of shoreless waters looked like blood.

Then the Moon came up, quite in her wrong position, very close to the sun, and she also looked red. And at the sight of her the sun began shooting out great flames, like whiskers or snakes of crimson fire, towards her. It is as if he were an octopus trying to draw her to himself in his tentacles. And perhaps he did draw her. At any rate she came to him, slowly at first, but then more and more quickly, till at last his long flames licked round her and the two ran together and became one huge ball like a burning coal. Great lumps of fire came dropping out of it into the sea and clouds of steam rose up.

Then Aslan said, "Now make an end."

The giant threw his horn into the sea. Then he stretched out one arm – very black it looked, and thousands of miles long – across the sky till his hand reached the Sun. He took the Sun and squeezed it in his hand as you would squeeze an orange. And instantly there was total darkness.

Everyone except Aslan jumped back from the ice-cold air which now blew through the Doorway. Its edges were already covered with icicles.

"Peter, High King of Narnia," said Aslan. "Shut the Door."

Peter, shivering with cold, leaned out into the darkness and pulled the Door to. It scraped over ice as he pulled it. Then, rather clumsily (for even in that moment his hands had gone numb and blue) he took out a golden key and locked it.

They had seen strange things enough through that Doorway. But it was stranger than any of them to look round and find themselves in warm daylight, the blue sky above them, flowers at their feet, and laughter in Aslan's eyes.

He turned swiftly round, crouched lower, lashed himself with his tail and shot away like a golden arrow.

"Come further in! Come further up!" he shouted over his shoulder. But who could keep up with him at that pace? They set out walking Westward to follow him.

"So," said Peter, "night falls on Narnia. What, Lucy! You're not *crying*? With Aslan ahead, and all of us here?"

"Don't try to stop me, Peter," said Lucy, "I am sure Aslan would not. I am sure it is not wrong to mourn for Narnia. Think of all that lies dead and frozen behind that door."

"Yes and I *did* hope," said Jill, "that it might go on for ever. I knew *our* world couldn't. I did think Narnia might."

"I saw it begin," said the Lord Digory. "I did not think I would live to see it die."

"Sirs," said Tirian. "The ladies do well to weep. See, I do so myself. I have seen my mother's death. What world but Narnia have I ever known? It were no virtue, but great discourtesy, if we did not mourn."

They walked away from the Door and away from the Dwarfs who still sat crowded together in their imaginary stable. And as they went they talked to one another about old wars and old peace and ancient Kings and all the glories of Narnia.

The Dogs were still with them. They joined in the conversation but not much because they were too busy racing on ahead and racing back and rushing off to sniff at smells in the grass till they made themselves sneeze. Suddenly they picked up a scent which seemed to excite them very much. They all started arguing about it — "Yes it is — No it isn't — That's just what I said — anyone can smell what *that* is — Take your great nose out of the way and let someone else smell."

"What is it, cousins?" said Peter.

"A Calormene, Sire," said several Dogs at once.

"Lead on to him, then," said Peter. "Whether he meets us in peace or war, he shall be welcome."

The Dogs darted on ahead and came back a moment later, running as if their lives depended on it, and barking loudly to say that it really was a Calormene. (Talking Dogs, just like the common ones, behave as if they thought whatever they are doing at the moment immensely important.)

The others followed where the Dogs led them and found a young Calormene sitting under a chestnut tree beside a clear stream of water. It was Emeth. He rose at once and bowed gravely.

"Sir," he said to Peter, "I know not whether you are my friend or my foe, but I should count it my honour to have you for either. Has not one of the poets said that a

noble friend is the best gift and a noble enemy the next
best?"

"Sir," said Peter, "I do not know that there need be any
war between you and us."

"Do tell us who you are and what's happened to you,"
said Jill.

"If there's going to be a story, let's all have a drink and
sit down," barked the Dogs. "We're quite blown."

"Well of course you will be if you keep tearing about
the way you have done," said Eustace.

So the humans sat down on the grass. And when the
Dogs had all had a very noisy drink out of the stream they
all sat down, bolt upright, panting, with their tongues
hanging out of their heads a little on one side to hear the
story. But Jewel remained standing, polishing his horn
against his side.

CHAPTER FIFTEEN

FURTHER UP AND FURTHER IN

"Know, O Warlike Kings," said Emeth, "and you, O ladies whose beauty illuminates the universe, that I am Emeth the seventh son of Harpha Tarkaan of the city of Tehishbaan, Westward beyond the desert. I came lately into Narnia with nine and twenty others under the command of Rishda Rarkaan. Now when I first heard that we should march upon Narnia I rejoiced; for I had heard many things of your Land and desired greatly to meet you in battle. But when I found that we were to go in disguised as merchants (which is a shameful dress for a warrior and the son of a Tarkaan) and to work by lies and trickery, then my joy departed from me. And most of all when I found we must wait upon a Monkey, and when it began to be said that Tash and Aslan were one, then the world became dark in my eyes. For always since I was a boy I have served Tash and my great desire was to know more of him, if it might be, to look upon his face. But the name of Aslan was hateful to me.

"And, as you have seen, we were called together outside the straw-roofed hovel, night after night, and the fire was kindled, and the Ape brought forth out of the hovel something upon four legs that I could not well see. And the people and the Beasts bowed down and did honour to it. But I thought, the Tarkaan is deceived by the Ape: for this thing that comes out of the stable is neither Tash nor any other god. But when I watched the Tarkaan's face, and marked every word that he said to the Monkey, then I changed my mind: for I saw that the Tarkaan did not believe in it himself. And then I understood that he did not believe in Tash at all: for if he had, how could he dare to mock him?

"When I understood this, a great rage fell upon me and I wondered that the true Tash did not strike down both the Monkey and the Tarkaan with fire from heaven. Nevertheless I hid my anger and held my tongue and waited to see how it would end. But last night, as some of you know, the Monkey brought not forth the yellow thing but said that all who desired to look upon Tashlan – for so they mixed the two words to pretend that they were all one – must pass one by one into the hovel. And I said to myself, Doubtless this is some other deception. But when the Cat had followed in and had come out again in a madness of terror, then I said to myself, Surely the true Tash, whom they called on without knowledge or belief, has now come among us, and will avenge himself. And though my heart was turned into water inside me because of the greatness and terror of Tash, yet my desire was stronger than my fear, and I put force upon my knees to stay them from trembling, and on my teeth that they should not chatter, and resolved to look upon the face of Tash though he should slay me. So I offered myself to go into the hovel; and the Tarkaan, though unwillingly, let me go.

"As soon as I had gone in at the door, the first wonder was that I found myself in this great sunlight (as we all are now) though the inside of the hovel had looked dark from outside. But I had no time to marvel at this, for immediately I was forced to fight for my head against one of our own men. As soon as I saw him I understood that the Monkey and the Tarkaan had set him there to slay any who came in if he were not in their secrets: so that this man also was a liar and a mocker and no true servant of Tash. I had the better will to fight him; and having slain the villain, I cast him out behind me through the door.

"Then I looked about me and saw the sky and the wide lands, and smelled the sweetness. And I said, By the Gods, this is a pleasant place: it may be that I am come into the country of Tash. And I began to journey into the strange country and to seek him.

"So I went over much grass and many flowers and among all kinds of wholesome and delectable trees till lo! in a narrow place between two rocks there came to meet me a great Lion. The speed of him was like the ostrich, and his size was an elephant's; his hair was like pure gold and the brightness of his eyes like gold that is liquid in the furnace. He was more terrible than the Flaming Mountain of Lagour, and in beauty he surpassed all that is in the world even as the rose in bloom surpasses the dust of the desert. Then I fell at his feet and thought, Surely this is the hour of death, for the Lion (who is worthy of all honour) will know that I have served Tash all my days and not him. Nevertheless, it is better to see the Lion and die than to be Tisroc of the world and live and not to have seen him. But the Glorious One bent down his golden head and touched my forehead with his tongue and said, Son, thou art welcome. But I said, Alas, Lord, I am no son of thine but the servant of Tash. He answered, Child, all the service thou hast done to Tash, I account as service done to me. Then by reasons of my great desire for wisdom and understanding, I overcame my fear and questioned the Glorious One and said, Lord, is it then true, as the Ape said, that thou and Tash are one? The Lion growled so that the earth shook (but his wrath was not against me) and said, It is false. Not because he and I are one, but because we are opposites, I take to me the services which thou hast done to him. For I and he are of such different kinds that no service which is vile can be done to me, and none which is not vile can be done to him. Therefore if any man swear by Tash and keep his oath for the oath's sake, it is by me that he has truly sworn, though he know it not, and it is I who reward him. And if any man do a cruelty in my name, then, though he says the name Aslan, it is Tash whom he serves and by Tash his deed is accepted. Dost thou understand, Child? I said, Lord, thou knowest how much I understand. But I said also (for the truth constrained me), Yet I have been seeking Tash all my days. Beloved, said the Glorious One, unless thy desire had been for me thou wouldst not have sought so long and so truly. For all find what they truly seek.

"Then he breathed upon me and took away the trembling from my limbs and caused me to stand upon my feet. And after that, he said not much, but that we should meet again, and I must go further up and further in. Then he turned him about in a storm and flurry of gold and was gone suddenly.

"And since then, O Kings and Ladies, I have been wandering to find him and my happiness is so great that it even weakens me like a wound. And this is the marvel of marvels, that he called me Beloved, me who am but as a dog –"

"Eh? What's that?" said one of the Dogs.

"Sir," said Emeth. "It is but a fashion of speech which we have in Calormen."

"Well, I can't say it's one I like very much," said the Dog.

"He doesn't mean any harm," said an older Dog.

"After all, *we* call our puppies *Boys* when they don't behave properly."

"So we do," said the first Dog. "Or *girls*."

"S-s-sh!" said the Old Dog. "That's not a nice word to use. Remember where you are."

"Look!" said Jill suddenly. Someone was coming, rather timidly, to meet them; a graceful creature on four feet, all silvery-grey. And they stared at him for a whole ten seconds before five or six voices said all at once, "Why, it's old Puzzle!" They had never seen him by daylight with the lion-skin off, and it made an extraordinary difference. He was himself now: a beautiful donkey with such a soft, grey coat and such a gentle, honest face that if you had seen him you would have done just what Jill and Lucy did – rushed forward and put your arms round his neck and kissed his nose and stroked his ears.

When they asked him where he had been he said he had

come in at the door along with all the other creatures but he had – well, to tell the truth, he had been keeping out of their way as much as he could; and out of Aslan's way. For the sight of the real Lion had made him so ashamed of all that nonsense about dressing up in a lion-skin that he did not know how to look anyone in the face. But when he saw that all his friends were going away Westward, and after he had had a mouthful of grass ("And I've never tasted such good grass in my life," said Puzzle), he plucked up his courage and followed. "But what I'll do if I really have to meet Aslan, I'm sure I don't know," he added.

"You'll find it will be all right when you really do," said Queen Lucy.

Then they went forward together, always Westward, for that seemed to be the direction Aslan had meant when he cried out, "Further up and futher in." Many other creatures were slowly moving the same way, but that grassy country was very wide and there was no crowding.

It still seemed to be early, and the morning freshness was in the air. They kept on stopping to look round and to look behind them, partly because it was so beautiful but partly also because there was something about it which they could not understand.

"Peter," said Lucy, "where is this, do you suppose?"

"I don't know," said the High King. "It reminds me of somewhere but I can't give it a name. Could it be somewhere we once stayed for a holiday when we were very, very small?"

"It would have to have been a jolly good holiday," said Eustace. "I bet there isn't a country like this anywhere in *our* world. Look at the colours! You couldn't get a blue like the blue on those mountains in our world."

"Is it not Aslan's country?" said Tirian.

"Not like Aslan's country on top of that mountain beyond the Eastern end of the world," said Jill. "I've been there."

"If you ask me," said Edmund, "it's like somewhere in the Narnian world. Look at those mountains ahead – and the big ice-mountains beyond them. Surely they're rather like the mountains we used to see from Narnia, the ones up Westward beyond the Waterfall?"

"Yes, so they are," said Peter. "Only these are bigger."

"I don't think *those* ones are so very like anything in Narnia," said Lucy. "But look there." She pointed Southward to their left, and everyone stopped and turned to look. "Those hills," said Lucy, "the nice woody ones and the blue ones behind – aren't they very like the Southern border of Narnia?"

"Like!" cried Edmund after a moment's silence. "Why, they're exactly like. Look, there's Mount Pire with his forked head, and there's the pass into Archenland and everything!"

"And yet they're not like," said Lucy. "They're different. They have more colours on them and they look further away than I remembered and they're more ... more ... oh, I don't know ..."

"More like the real thing," said the Lord Digory softly.

Suddenly Farsight the Eagle spread his wings, soared

thirty or forty feet up into the air, circled round and then alighted on the ground.

"Kings and Queens," he cried, "we have all been blind. We are only beginning to see where we are. From up there I have seen it all – Ettinsmuir, Beaversdam, the Great River, and Cair Paravel still shining on the edge of the Eastern Sea. Narnia is not dead. This is Narnia."

"But how can it be?" said Peter. "For Aslan told us older ones that we should never return to Narnia, and here we are."

"Yes," said Eustace. "And we saw it all destroyed and the sun put out."

"And it's all so different," said Lucy.

"The Eagle is right," said the Lord Digory. "Listen, Peter. When Aslan said you could never go back to Narnia, he meant the Narnia you were thinking of. But that was not the real Narnia. That had a beginning and an end. It was only a shadow or a copy of the real Narnia which has always been here and always will be here: just as our world, England and all, is only a shadow or copy of something in Aslan's real world. You need not mourn over Narnia, Lucy. All of the old Narnia that mattered, all the dear creatures, have been drawn into the real Narnia through the Door. And of course it is different;

as different as a real thing is from a shadow or as waking life is from a dream." His voice stirred everyone like a trumpet as he spoke these words: but when he added under his breath "It's all in Plato, all in Plato: bless me, what *do* they teach them at these schools!" the older ones laughed. It was so exactly like the sort of thing they had heard him say long ago in that other world where his beard was grey instead of golden. He knew why they were laughing and joined in the laugh himself. But very quickly they all became grave again: for, as you know, there is a kind of happiness and wonder that makes you serious. It is too good to waste on jokes.

It is as hard to explain how this sunlit land was different from the old Narnia as it would be to tell you how the fruits of that country taste. Perhaps you will get some idea of it if you think like this. You may have been in a room in which there was a window that looked out on a lovely bay of the sea or a green valley that wound away among mountains. And in the wall of that room opposite to the window there may have been a looking-glass. And as you turned away from the window you suddenly caught sight of that sea or that valley, all over again, in the looking glass. And the sea in the mirror, or the valley in the mirror, were in one sense just the same as the real ones: yet at the same time they were somehow different – deeper, more wonderful, more like places in a story: in a story you have never heard but very much want to know. The difference between the old Narnia and the new Narnia was like that. The new one was a deeper country: every rock and flower and blade of grass looked as if it meant more. I can't describe it any better than that: if ever you get there you will know what I mean.

It was the Unicorn who summed up what everyone was feeling. He stamped his right fore-hoof on the ground and neighed, and then cried:

"I have come home at last! This is my real country! I belong here. This is the land I have been looking for all my life, though I never knew it till now. The reason why we loved the old Narnia is that it sometimes looked a little like this. Bree-hee-hee! Come further up, come further in!"

He shook his mane and sprang forward into a great gallop – a Unicorn's gallop, which, in our world, would have carried him out of sight in a few moments. But now a most strange thing happened. Everyone else began to run, and they found, to their astonishment, that they could keep up with him: not only the Dogs and the humans but even fat little Puzzle and short-legged Poggin the Dwarf. The air flew in their faces as if they were driving fast in a car without a windscreen. The country flew past as if they were seeing it from the windows of an express train. Faster and faster they raced, but no one got hot or tired or out of breath.

CHAPTER SIXTEEN

FAREWELL TO SHADOWLANDS

IF one could run without getting tired, I don't think one would often want to do anything else. But there might be special reasons for stopping, and it was a special reason which made Eustace presently shout:

"I say! Steady! Look what we're coming to!"

And well he might. For now they saw before them Caldron Pool and beyond the Pool the high unclimbable cliffs and, pouring down the cliffs, thousands of tons of water every second, flashing like diamonds in some places and dark, glassy green in others, the Great Waterfall; and already the thunder of it was in their ears.

"Don't stop! Further up and further in," called Farsight, tilting his flight a little upwards.

"It's all very well for *him*," said Eustace, but Jewel also cried out:

"Don't stop. Further up and further in! Take it in your stride."

His voice could only just be heard above the roar of the water but next moment everyone saw that he had plunged into the Pool. And helter-skelter behind him, with splash after splash, all the others did the same. The water was not biting cold as all of them (and especially Puzzle) expected, but of a delicious foamy coolness. They all found they were swimming straight for the Waterfall itself.

"This is absolutely crazy," said Eustace to Edmund.

"I know. And yet –" said Edmund.

"Isn't it wonderful?" said Lucy. "Have you noticed one can't feel afraid, even if one wants to? Try it."

"By Jove, neither one can," said Eustace after he had tried.

Jewel reached the foot of the Waterfall first, but Tirian was only just behind him. Jill was last, so she could see the whole thing better than the others. She saw something white moving steadily up the face of the Waterfall. That white thing was the Unicorn. You couldn't tell whether he was swimming or climbing, but he moved on, higher and higher. The point of his horn divided the water just above his head, and it cascaded out in two rainbow-coloured streams all round his shoulders. Just behind him came King Tirian. He moved his legs and arms as if he were swimming but he moved straight upwards: as if one could swim up the wall of a house.

What looked funniest was the Dogs. During the gallop they had not been at all out of breath, but now, as they swarmed and wriggled upwards, there was plenty of spluttering and sneezing among them; that was because they would keep on barking, and every time they barked they got their mouths and noses full of water. But before Jill had time to notice all these things fully, she was going up the Waterfall herself. It was the sort of thing that would have been quite impossible in our world. Even if you hadn't been drowned, you would have been smashed to pieces by the terrible weight of water against the countless jags of rock. But in that world you could do it. You went on, up and up, with all kinds of reflected lights flashing at you from the water and all manner of coloured stones flashing through it, till it seemed as if you were climbing up light itself – and always higher and higher till the sense of height would have terrified you if you could be terrified, but later it was only gloriously exciting. And then at last one came to the lovely, smooth green curve in which the water poured over the top and found that one was out on the level river above the Waterfall. The current was racing away behind you, but you were such a wonderful swimmer that you could make headway against it. Soon they were all on the bank, dripping but happy.

A long valley opened ahead and great snow-mountains, now much nearer, stood up against the sky.

"Further up and further in," cried Jewel and instantly they were off again.

They were out of Narnia now and up into the Western Wild which neither Tirian nor Peter nor even the Eagle had ever seen before. But the Lord Digory and the Lady Polly had. "Do you remember? Do you remember?" they said – and said it in steady voices too, without panting, though the whole party was now running faster than an arrow flies.

"What, Lord?" said Tirian. "Is it then true, as stories tell, that you two journeyed here on the very day the world was made?"

"Yes," said Digory, "and it seems to me as if it were only yesterday."

"And on a flying horse?" asked Tirian. "Is that part true?"

"Certainly," said Digory. But the Dogs barked, "Faster, faster!"

So they ran faster and faster till it was more like flying than running, and even the Eagle overhead was going no faster than they. And they went through winding valley after winding valley and up the steep sides of hills and, faster than ever, down the other side, following the river and sometimes crossing it and skimming across mountain-lakes as if they were living speed-boats, till at last at the far end of one long lake which looked as blue as a turquoise, they saw a smooth green hill. Its sides were as steep as the sides of a pyramid and round the very top of it ran a green wall: but above the wall rose the branches of trees whose leaves looked like silver and their fruit like gold.

"Further up and further in!" roared the Unicorn, and no one held back. They charged straight at the foot of the hill and then found themselves running up it almost as water from a broken wave runs up a rock out at the point of some bay. Though the slope was nearly as steep as the roof of a house and the grass was smooth as a bowling green, no one slipped. Only when they had reached the very top did they slow up; that was because they found themselves facing great golden gates. And for a moment none of them was bold enough to try if the gates would open. They all felt just as they had felt about the fruit – "Dare we? Is it right? Can it be meant for *us*?"

But while they were standing thus a great horn, wonderfully loud and sweet, blew from somewhere inside that walled garden and the gates swung open.

Tirian stood holding his breath and wondering who would come out. And what came was the last thing he had expected: a little, sleek, bright-eyed Talking Mouse with a red feather stuck in a circlet on its head and its left paw resting on a long sword. It bowed, a most beautiful bow, and said in its shrill voice:

"Welcome, in the Lion's name. Come further up and further in."

Then Tirian saw King Peter and King Edmund and Queen Lucy rush forward to kneel down and greet the Mouse and they all cried out "Reepicheep!" And Tirian breathed fast with the sheer wonder of it, for now he

knew that he was looking at one of the great heroes of
Narnia, Reepicheep the Mouse who had fought at the
great Battle of Beruna and afterwards sailed to the
World's end with King Caspian the Seafarer. But before
he had had much time to think of this he felt two strong
arms thrown about him and felt a bearded kiss on his
cheeks and heard a well remembered voice saying:

"What, lad? Art thicker and taller since I last touched
thee!"

It was his own father, the good King Erlian: but not as
Tirian had seen him last when they brought him home
pale and wounded from his fight with the giant, nor even
as Tirian remembered him in his later years when he was
a grey-headed warrior. This was his father, young and
merry, as he could just remember him from very early
days when he himself had been a little boy playing games

with his father in the castle garden at Cair Paravel, just
before bedtime on summer evenings. The very smell of the
bread-and-milk he used to have for supper came back to
him.

Jewel thought to himself, "I will leave them to talk for
a little and then I will go and greet the good King Erlian.
Many a bright apple has he given me when I was but a
colt." But next moment he had something else to think of,
for out of the gateway there came a horse so mighty and
noble that even a Unicorn might feel shy in its presence: a
great winged horse. It looked a moment at the Lord
Digory and the Lady Polly and neighed out "What,
cousins!" and they both shouted "Fledge! Good old
Fledge!" and rushed to kiss it.

But by now the Mouse was again urging them to come
in. So all of them passed in through the golden gates, into
the delicious smell that blew towards them out of that
garden and into the cool mixture of sunlight and shadow
under the trees, walking on springy turf that was all
dotted with white flowers. The very first thing which
struck everyone was that the place was far larger than it
had seemed from outside. But no one had time to think
about that for people were coming up to meet the newcomers from every direction.

Everyone you had ever heard of (if you knew the history of these countries) seemed to be there. There was
Glimfeather the Owl and Puddleglum the Marshwiggle,
and King Rilian the Disenchanted, and his mother the
Star's daughter and his great father Caspian himself. And
close beside him were the Lord Drinian and the Lord
Berne and Trumpkin the Dwarf and Truffle-hunter the
good Badger with Glenstorm the Centaur and a hundred
other heroes of the great War of Deliverance. And then

from another side came Cor the King of Archenland with King Lune his father and his wife Queen Aravis and the brave prince Corin Thunder-Fist, his brother, and Bree the Horse and Hwin the Mare. And then – which was a wonder beyond all wonders to Tirian – there came from further away in the past, the two good Beavers and Tumnus the Faun. And there was greeting and kissing and hand-shaking and old jokes revived, (you've no idea how good an old joke sounds when you take it out again after a rest of five or six hundred years) and the whole company moved forward to the centre of the orchard where the Phoenix sat in a tree and looked down upon them all, and at the foot of that tree were two thrones and in those two thrones a King and Queen so great and beautiful that everyone bowed down before them. And well they might, for these two were King Frank and Queen Helen from whom all the most ancient Kings of Narnia and Archenland are descended. And Tirian felt as you would feel if you were brought before Adam and Eve in all their glory.

About half an hour later – or it might have been half a hundred years later, for time there is not like time here – Lucy stood with her dear friend, her oldest Narnian friend, the Faun Tumnus, looking down over the wall of that garden, and seeing all Narnia spread out below. But when you looked down you found that this hill was much higher than you had thought: it sank down with shining cliffs, thousands of feet below them and trees in that lower world looked no bigger than grains of green salt. Then she turned inward again and stood with her back to the wall and looked at the garden.

"I see," she said at last, thoughtfully. "I see now. This

garden is like the stable. It is far bigger inside than it was outside."

"Of course, Daughter of Eve," said the Faun. "The further up and the further in you go, the bigger everything gets. The inside is larger than the outside."

Lucy looked hard at the garden and saw that it was not really a garden but a whole world, with its own rivers and woods and sea and mountains. But they were not strange: she knew them all.

"I see," she said. "This is still Narnia, and more real and more beautiful then the Narnia down below, just as *it* was more real and more beautiful than the Narnia outside the stable door! I see ... world within world, Narnia within Narnia ..."

"Yes," said Mr Tumnus, "like an onion: except that as you go in and in, each circle is larger than the last."

And Lucy looked this way and that and soon found that a new and beautiful thing had happened to her. Whatever she looked at, however far away it might be, once she had fixed her eyes steadily on it, became quite clear and close as if she were looking through a telescope. She could see the whole Southern desert and beyond it the great city of Tashbaan: to Eastward she could see Cair Paravel on the edge of the sea and the very window of the room that had once been her own. And far out to sea she could discover the islands, islands after islands to the end of the world, and, beyond the end, the huge mountain which they had called Aslan's country. But now she saw that it was part of a great chain of mountains which ringed round the whole world. In front of her it seemed to come quite close. Then she looked to her left and saw what she took to be a great bank of brightly-coloured cloud, cut off from them by a gap. But she looked harder and saw that it was not a cloud at all but a real land. And when she had fixed her eyes on one particular spot of it, she at once cried out, "Peter! Edmund! Come and look! Come quickly." And they came and looked, for their eyes also had become like hers.

"Why!" exclaimed Peter. "It's England. And that's the house itself — Professor Kirk's old home in the country where all our adventures began!"

"I thought that house had been destroyed," said Edmund.

"So it was," said the Faun. "But you are now looking at the England within England, the real England just as this is the real Narnia. And in that inner England no good thing is destroyed."

Suddenly they shifted their eyes to another spot, and then Peter and Edmund and Lucy gasped with amazement and shouted out and began waving: for there they saw their own father and mother, waving back at them across the great, deep valley. It was like when you see people waving at you from the deck of a big ship when you are waiting on the quay to meet them.

"How can we get at them?" said Lucy.

"That is easy," said Mr Tumnus. "That country and this country — all the *real* countries — are only spurs jutting out from the great mountains of Aslan. We have only to walk along the ridge, upward and inward, till it joins on. And listen! There is King Frank's horn: we must all go up."

And soon they found themselves all walking together — and a great, bright procession it was — up towards mountains higher than you could see in this world even if they were there to be seen. But there was no snow on those mountains: there were forests and green slopes and sweet orchards and flashing waterfalls, one above the other, going up forever. And the land they were walking on grew narrower all the time, with a deep valley on each side: and across that valley the land which was the real England grew nearer and nearer.

The light ahead was growing stronger. Lucy saw that a great series of many-coloured cliffs led up in front of them like a giant's staircase. And then she forgot everything else, because Aslan himself was coming, leaping down from cliff to cliff like a living cataract of power and beauty.

And the very first person whom Aslan called to him was Puzzle the Donkey. You never saw a donkey look feebler and sillier than Puzzle did as he walked up to Aslan, and he looked, beside Aslan, as small as a kitten looks beside a St Bernard. The Lion bowed down his head and whispered something to Puzzle at which his long ears went down, but then he said something else at which the ears perked up again. The humans couldn't hear what he had said either time. Then Aslan turned to them and said:

"You do not yet look so happy as I mean you to be."

Lucy said, "We're so afraid of being sent away, Aslan. And you have sent us back into our own world so often."

"No fear of that," said Aslan. "Have you not guessed?"

Their hearts leaped and a wild hope rose within them.

"There *was* a real railway accident," said Aslan softly. "Your father and mother and all of you are — as you used to call it in the Shadowlands — dead. The term is over: the holidays have begun. The dream is ended: this is the morning."

And as He spoke He no longer looked to them like a lion; but the things that began to happen after that were so great and beautiful that I cannot write them. And for us this is the end of all the stories, and we can most truly say that they all lived happily ever after. But for them it was only the beginning of the real story. All their life in this world and all their adventures in Narnia had only been the cover and the title page: now at last they were beginning Chapter One of the Great Story which no one on earth has read: which goes on forever: in which every chapter is better than the one before.